The Sheltered Life of Betsy Parker

2nd edition

E. David Hopkins

For Kristen

ISBN-13: 978-1537047126

ISBN-10: 1537047124

Publisher: CreateSpace, 2016

Library of Congress Control Number: 2016914079
CreateSpace Independent Publishing Platform, North Charleston, SC

Cover design by Gourav Shah, with words and picture edited by Ted Hopkins

© E. David Hopkins

To Ted, Tina and Angela
To James, Garth and Stephen
To all the loving people in my naturist community
To Gareth and Zoe
To Marisa, Darrell, Devyn, Richard and Olivia
To Jim and Cathy
To Darren Groth, a local author, who served as a valuable helper to make this book publishable

Table of Contents

1 A Late-summer Romance

It was August 31. Carl Parker was sitting under a big Beech Tree, in Lilly Park, in a town called Meriton, soaking up the late-summer sunshine. The warm air was carrying the first mellow tinge of autumn, swaying a few leaves on the tree, and caressing Carl in a loving, tender, natural embrace.

As Carl relaxed in the sun, he was thinking about what the finest attire could be that would attract a woman. He had always felt nervous around women. Every time Carl had met someone with whom he felt he could build a relationship, he had never felt the confidence, nor the readiness to proceed.

As Carl was focussing on the current trend, trying to think of the optimum suit that would please a woman, he heard someone sit down at the other side of the tree and he jumped to his feet with a start.

"No need to be scared," a voice replied with a chuckle. It was a female's voice; a young woman, about Carl's age.

Carl turned to the other side of the tree, and found an attractive girl sitting just as he had been, gazing up into the leaves of the tree.

Carl didn't know how to respond. "Hi there," he smiled sort of timidly. "Beautiful day isn't it? Not going to be many more like them. Might as well enjoy the last bit of summer while you can."

"Oh, don't be so negative. It's still August," the girl commented. "We've got a good few weeks of warm weather ahead of us. Besides, summer always comes around every year. It's not like it's the last summer on the face of the Earth."

"I know," Carl chuckled, "but summer always takes forever to come around again. What brings you out?"

“It was just such a mellow, warm day, I had to catch the sun's rays,” she paused, “under this gorgeous Beech Tree.”

“That's just how I feel,” Carl replied. “Do you consider yourself into fashion?”

“No!” Carl thought. “There I go again; asking another personal question to someone I don't even know.”

However, much to Carl's relief, the girl answered with a sincere smile. “Well, I don't give a whole lot of thought about fashion, but I do enjoy the classy dress now and again.”

“I'm not really a fashion guy,” Carl grinned sheepishly. “I was just hoping to know what the current trend was. Just my curiosity I suppose.”

“Well, I wouldn't dwell too much on it,” the girl chuckled. “Name's Megan, by the way. Megan Willow. How do you like that?”

“I'm Carl ... Carl Parker,” Carl replied.

Carl Parker had always thought his name, particularly his first and last name together, sounded rather odd. Therefore, he rarely introduced himself to anyone as “Carl Parker” and had taken to introducing himself as simply “Carl,” but this girl seemed so happy and kind that Carl saw it fit to introduce himself by both his first and last name.

“I like that,” Megan smiled, “Carl Parker,” she whispered to herself.

Carl was pleased at how sincere Megan's tone was. He turned to Megan and asked, “Hey, can we go grab dinner at Nico the Greek?”

“I would love that,” Megan nodded.

***

From then on, a whirlwind romance developed. That one simple date turned into more conversation, which turned into more dates, which turned into the two seeing each other almost all the time, which turned into marriage, on August 31, exactly one year after they had met under the tree.

On their second wedding anniversary, Carl and Megan were enjoying a sumptuous meal at that same Greek restaurant where they'd eaten that first dinner on the day they'd met. Carl was eating chicken souvlaki with rice, and Megan was enjoying moussaka.

Not only were they enjoying their favorite dinner on their second wedding anniversary, they were also expecting their first child. Megan was due to give birth in four-and-a-half months.

“What will her name be?” Megan smiled to her husband.

“What makes you think it will be a girl?” Carl chuckled. “It's got just as good a chance to be a boy.”

“Oh I don't know. I'm the mother and I can feel it. So, what should we name her?”

“How about Anne, or Susan, or Judith?” Carl suggested.

“Oh no!” Megan cried. “Nothing like that. A girl should have a name that carries dignity, that sounds sweet, that feels pleasant and soft on the tongue.”

Megan paused in thought for a few moments before she spoke again.

“I have always adored the name 'Elizabeth' but it's not used so much nowadays. Seems a terrible shame.”

“Then why don't we name her 'Elizabeth?'” Carl asked, but his wife wasn't really listening anymore. She was off in her own world savoring this sweet name she had in her head.

“And you know what else?” she continued. “There are so many fascinating ways to abbreviate Elizabeth; I suspect more than any other name in the world: there's Liz, Lizzy, Eliza, Tess, Tessa,

Beth, Bess, Bessie, Betty and," she paused again "Betsy, such a cool combination of those last two."

"So you want to name our daughter Betsy?" Carl asked dumbfounded. He didn't think 'Betsy' sounded any more dignified, sweet or princessly than any of the names he had suggested. "That is if our baby is even a daughter at all."

"Sure I do. Betsy Parker. That sounds grand, doesn't it?"

"I suppose it does," Carl smiled. He was surprised that his wife had settled on a name so quickly, one he thought he'd have never considered even if he'd had a lifetime to think about it, but he decided that 'Betsy Parker' had a fine ring to it all the same. "Very well. We will name our baby Betsy then."

Then, Carl paused in thought, "And what if it happens to be a boy?"

Megan looked pensive for a moment, and made a sigh as though she had been beaten at her own game. Then, her expression turned into a joyous, laughing smile once again.

"I thought up a good girl's name; I will leave you to think up a good boy's name," Megan beamed at her husband.

"I will do that," Carl smiled, as they polished off their dinners.

2 The Rash

On January 16, at four o'clock in the morning, Megan Parker went into labor. Her husband drove her to the hospital, and, three hours later, she gave birth to a baby girl.

"There you go, Megan," the nurse smiled as he handed Megan her baby, wrapped in a pink cloth. "You have been blessed with a healthy, beautiful baby girl."

"Well blow me down," Carl breathed in awe. "You were right Megan. It's a girl. Betsy Parker it is."

The couple gazed at their new daughter in amazement and admiration. She had some strands of light blonde hair, and she already looked happy, eager, and ready to live a full life. Both her parents were delighted, but nervous as well, as they had never raised a child before.

"I'm happy it's a girl," Megan smiled, "but I'm even more happy that it's healthy."

"Boy, girl, healthy or unhealthy, it's a blessing all the same," Carl replied in awe, "Just as long as she lives her life as a caring, wonderful person."

"I couldn't have said it better," smiled Megan.

"We'll keep her in the hospital for a few days," said nurse Ken Reynolds, "This is just to look after her while she is in her first days, and make sure nothing unusual develops."

The first two days of Betsy's life at the hospital passed swimmingly. She was a happy, calm, bright-eyed baby who rarely cried, and Megan was able to breastfeed Betsy well.

On January 18, the couple were able to bring their new daughter home, where they already had a crib, yellow wallpaper, an airplane mobile, diapers, and a wide assortment of clothes set up for her.

On January 26, Carl and Megan brought Betsy to church to have her baptized and Christened. The minister was a friendly man named Ben Herb, who was proud that The Lord had sent this lovely young couple in his congregation a baby girl, and he was determined to declare baby Betsy dedicated to Christ.

For the first month of Betsy's life, the couple looked after their daughter like any parents do. She couldn't play yet, but she looked around at people and objects. By day, her parents watched over her, changed her diapers, and her mother breastfed her. By night, her parents bathed her, and put her to bed in her crib. The care they provided for Betsy was becoming a daily routine. Both her parents longed for and anticipated the days when Betsy would be able to laugh, walk, talk, play, watch fun TV shows, meet other children, and take part in so many childhood activities.

On March 1, when Betsy was a month-and-a-half old, her parents woke up in the night to their daughter crying.

“Oh, she just needs her diaper changing. I'll take care of it Megan,” mumbled Carl, as he stumbled out of bed.

He made his way into Betsy's room, where the baby was indeed upset about something. Carl picked Betsy up, and looked her over. Then, he checked under Betsy's diaper.

“Oh dear,” he breathed, “It's diaper rash. I'll go grab the anti-rash cream.”

Carl took Betsy to the bathroom, and applied the cream.

“There you go,” he assured the infant, “it will soon feel better.”

He carried Betsy back to her crib, and put her under the sheets.

“I think I'd better keep an eye on her for the next little while till she settles down,” thought Carl.

As Carl watched over his daughter, he was starting to sense that something was wrong. Betsy's crying wasn't going away. If anything, it was getting worse. He picked Betsy up, and checked the rash once more. It was more angry than before, and was starting to spread. He hurried and got Megan.

“Something's happening,” Carl told Megan. “I think Betsy might be sick.”

Megan got out of bed. “What seems to be the problem?” she asked.

“This 'diaper rash' I mentioned is getting angrier and is starting to spread.”

When both parents arrived at Betsy's crib, something was definitely wrong. Betsy's crying was louder, and the rash had spread over her chest, abdomen and legs.

“I think it's chickenpox,” Megan cried out, petrified. “We have to take her to the hospital now.”

“If it were chickenpox, she would have a fever,” Carl insisted. He felt Betsy's forehead. “Her temperature is normal.”

“We're taking her to the hospital,” Megan insisted, “chickenpox or not, there is something very wrong with her.”

The parents bundled into the car and put Betsy in her car seat. Then, they drove her to the hospital. When they arrived, the triage nurse looked across her desk at the parents and the crying baby.

“So what seems to be the problem?” she asked.

“Betsy woke up with a rash,” Carl told her. “I thought it was diaper rash; we treated it, but the rash didn't go away. It's spread over most of Betsy's body. Is it chickenpox? Will she need to be kept in isolation?”

“Take a seat in the waiting room,” the triage nurse replied. “A doctor will be with you shortly.”

After an intense stay in the waiting room, Carl and Megan heard footsteps approaching.

“Hey there,” a voice called out. Carl and Megan looked

towards the voice. A doctor had arrived. "My name is Dr. Derek Crown. Come with me. We will see what's wrong with Betsy."

The couple followed the doctor down the hall, into a hospital room. Upon arriving at this room, the doctor laid Betsy on a bed. He looked the baby over.

"It's not chickenpox," he observed, "and it's nothing else viral either, or bacterial for that matter. It appears to be an allergic reaction."

"But what could Betsy be allergic to?" Megan cried. "Whatever it is, we are getting rid of it, once and for all."

"You say it started under the diaper, and it looked like diaper rash?"

"Yes," Carl acknowledged.

"And when you applied cream, the rash didn't go away?"

"No, it didn't."

"Then," the doctor paused, "if it started under the diaper, and cream didn't help, and this appears to be an allergic reaction then, maybe, just maybe, she's allergic to the diaper itself. Would you mind if I take her diaper off?"

"Go ahead," Carl assured him, "anything that would make Betsy better."

The doctor undid the velcro and removed the diaper. Then, he looked the diaper over.

"It appears to be made of cotton," he observed. "Some people are allergic to cotton. Your baby must have a cotton allergy. From now on, I would recommend using plastic diapers."

"She has always been wearing cotton diapers," Carl said, "and it's never been a problem up until now."

"Well, sometimes allergies take a long time to develop."

Within the next few hours, Betsy was making a stunning recovery. However, the parents and the doctor noticed one peculiarity. Underneath Betsy's shirt, the rash lingered, and this irritated the baby. It wasn't particularly threatening to Betsy's health but it concerned her parents.

"Could she be allergic to her shirt too?" Carl asked dumbfounded.

"Maybe," the doctor replied.

Carl removed Betsy's shirt, leaving their baby naked on the hospital bed.

In another hour, the rash was gone completely and Betsy had returned to normal.

"Thank you!" Megan cried. "But what should our daughter wear?"

"Give her plastic diapers," the doctor said, "and here."

The doctor whipped out a slip of paper and scribbled something on it.

"This is an antihistamine cream. Use it on your daughter right away if ever there is a similar reaction in the future. She should be fine wearing the kinds of shirts that she does now, as long as you use this cream, but I urge you to no longer use any cotton on her. Just pick up the prescription from the pharmacy first thing in the morning."

"Thank you for your help," Megan smiled at the doctor.

***

The first thing, the next morning, when the stores were opening, Carl drove into town and bought a box of plastic diapers for Betsy, and the cream the doctor had prescribed. He put a diaper on Betsy, put the cream on her chest, and put her shirt back on.

Happy and relieved, Carl and Megan smiled at their daughter that she was healthy once again.

3 A Unique Diagnosis

From that night on, Betsy was healthy; for the next seven-and-a-half months at least. Carl and Megan put the cream on her, dressed her in plastic diapers, and marvelled at how well and happy Betsy was.

And then, one night in the middle of October, when Betsy was nine months old, Carl and Megan were startled awake by screaming. It was worse than before and terrified the life out of Carl and Megan. They burst of out bed and hurried into Betsy's room.

"What's happening?!" Carl cried, picking up his daughter.

Underneath Betsy's diaper, and under her shirt was the most glaring rash her parents had ever seen. Betsy's crying was accompanied by wheezing and gurgling noises.

"We have to call an ambulance!" cried Megan. "You watch Betsy. I'm getting to the phone now!"

Megan sprinted out of Betsy's room, picked up the phone and dialled 911. "Please dispatch an ambulance!" Megan cried over the phone. "My address is 9635 82 Street" She threw the phone back into the holder.

Megan ran back into Betsy's room. By now, the girl had vomited!

"Get her clothes off!" Megan cried.

"What?" cried Carl. Then, a morbid thought raced across his mind. This was no ordinary baby; he could feel it. He then muttered, "Oh!" He turned back to his wife, but she was already removing Betsy's diaper and shirt.

Then, they looked at their daughter, who was swollen all over and had all sorts of hideous colors. Her skin looked like that of an alien from some exotic planet. On the spot, Betsy vomited again.

"I put her antihistamine lotion on before we put her to bed, I really did," Carl told his wife.

"I know you did dear. I saw you do it. I was there too."

There came a knock at the door. Carl ran over and answered it. Outside was an ambulance and two paramedics.

"Come with us, all of you," one of the medics told the Parkers. "We will take you and your baby to the hospital."

The medics took Betsy to the ambulance. After they had loaded Betsy inside, the parents sat in the back seat. Then, they departed.

As they drove along, they watched the black night scenery flash past. It was like watching Betsy's life, their beloved daughter's world, flashing away. A terrible dread was sinking into Carl and Megan, a dread that, if it were true, would wreck Betsy's whole life, forever, if she survived this episode.

Megan turned to Carl, "I think this is it."

Carl turned to Megan, "I think this is it too." Then, his gaze lingered upon his wife and he paused, "Whatever 'it' is."

"What do you mean?" stuttered Megan, although she knew too.

Carl shook his head. "I don't know how our daughter's life is going to work out. If Betsy survives this reaction she can never ever wear clothes again."

Megan looked her husband in the eyes, "I know dear," she cried. "And she'd become a hermit; she'd have to be. She'll never know human society, never meet anyone; never find anyone who loves her, or even respects her. She'll be the naked girl no one ever sees, and she'll never see anyone..." Megan paused, gazing at Carl, "except us."

At last they arrived at the hospital. The paramedics carried Betsy out and her parents followed. They carried Betsy to a room where a doctor worked. As a matter of fact, it was the very same doctor the family had seen months before.

"Betsy Parker again, is it?" he asked, as he looked at the swollen baby.

Carl nodded in a nervous, agitated manner. "Dr. Crown!" he cried. "What can we do? We've done everything we could to look after her. We even used plastic diapers and applied the cream you prescribed."

"I understand that," he replied. He looked at the hospital bed; then he looked at the baby as though he, himself, was unsure of what to do.

"She's definitely going to take at least a few days to recover," he explained. "She will have to remain in the hospital all that time."

One minute later, Betsy was laid down on the hospital bed, with an intravenous pumping antihistamine into her. Her crying gradually slowed, but it was still loud and her health was still at stake.

The doctor sat her up on the bed so that less of her skin would come into contact with the sheets. Later, when this was making some, but not very much, difference, he held Betsy in his hands, and turned to the parents.

"She seems to be allergic to almost everything," the doctor told them. "How much has she developed in her motor skills?"

"She's been able to hold things for a few weeks now," Carl explained. "The other morning, we noticed her trying to hold herself up by grabbing onto one of the bars of her crib."

The doctor thought for another minute. Then, he positioned Betsy to stand on her feet, and guided her hands to clasp the bedside railing. It was the darnedest thing the parents, the doctor, and possibly anyone had ever seen; a naked nine-month-old baby, with a nasty rash all over her, positioned by a doctor to stand on a hospital bed and hold onto the railing.

But nobody was laughing; not the doctor, and certainly not Betsy's parents.

"Come here," Dr. Crown motioned. Carl and Megan listened intently to the doctor.

"It appears your daughter has a peculiar kind of allergic reaction that affects her on the exterior. Perhaps, anything that touches her skin could spark an allergic reaction just like the one you have seen tonight, and threaten her very life."

"Has this ever happened before?" Carl asked, "on a person's outside?"

"I have never seen it, nor heard of it," he said. "I will do some digging, make some contacts in my medical group, and do some research to see if this has ever happened before. It could be that your daughter is truly unique. I don't know of any name for her condition, as I have never observed it before, and it quite possibly will never happen to anyone again."

"Oh, I hope it never happens to anyone again," stuttered Megan. "But what about our daughter? What will we do about her?"

For once, even the doctor was lost for words. He didn't answer the question. He simply stood there, in deep thought, considering Betsy's condition, and what the outcome would be from everything her parents could possibly do.

At last, he sighed, "I'm sorry. So so sorry." Then he returned to silence.

For a long time, nobody said a word. Carl and Megan's worst fear had been realized. The doctor's diagnosis had ended everything. They looked at their victimized, defenceless daughter. Her skin was showing the first signs of getting better, but Carl and Megan couldn't think of any way their daughter would ever be happy.

Megan turned to the doctor once again, in hope that this extensive period of contemplation would have put some kind of idea in his mind; something that would give Carl and Megan at least a molecule of hope. “What can we do to help Betsy?”

The doctor looked at the couple again, and said, just as before, “Carl and Megan. I am so sorry.”

“No!” the mother insisted. “That doesn't help! What are we going to do?”

The doctor sighed again, and another moment of silence passed. Finally he spoke.

“As long as Betsy keeps having these allergic reactions, you will have to keep her inside at all times,” he explained. “She will never be able to go anywhere in public. You will have to homeschool her. Keep an epi-pen with you at all times. I'm really sorry, both of you, but your daughter will be a hermit. You will have to be very careful with her, and she'll never be able to meet any other children.”

“She can't stay inside forever!” protested Carl. “It will ruin her! It will destroy her life!”

“I'm sorry,” explained the doctor, “but the law is the law. You take her out in public naked, and nobody's going to understand. People will stare at your daughter; people will turn away in embarrassment. You will get arrested for indecent exposure.”

“We can take it to court!” Carl cried. “We can fight the law, tooth and nail. Nobody is shutting our Betsy away; not now, not ever!”

“I wouldn't recommend it,” replied the doctor, “Legally, or societally, you will lose. Certain cultural attitudes are set in stone. Even if you take it to court and win, not everyone is going to understand. In fact, I wouldn't be surprised if most people don't.”

Carl and Megan looked once again at Betsy, whose rash was starting to fade. It appeared that her condition was stable, and she would make it through this reaction alive.

"I think I have done what I can for tonight," the doctor told the parents. "If you have any more questions, I can bring in a nurse."

"Thank you," Megan smiled. "That would be most helpful."

As the doctor left, Carl continued to position Betsy in the same way that the doctor had been.

A few minutes later, a nurse, by the name of Sheila, entered the room, and the doctor left.

"Will she ever get over this allergy?" Megan asked. "Will she ever be able to wear clothing and live life like a normal person?"

"There is no way we can predict what will come of Betsy's situation at this stage," the nurse said. "We will have to see."

"All the same, we have to give her a chance," said Megan. "Even if Betsy will never be happy, loved, understood, or cared for by anyone except ourselves, we have to take care of her in the best way we can. She is our daughter; we brought her into the world and it is up to us to give her at least a chance at life."

"Of course it is, and of course you love her," the nurse replied.

"What about water?" Carl asked. "Will we be able to at least bathe our daughter?"

"Water should be fine," the nurse explained. "The human body is 70% water. Betsy's skin attacks anything that is foreign to it, and water wouldn't be foreign."

"What about her feet and hands? Will she get really sick just by walking or holding anything?"

"I can't make any promises, as I believe nobody on Earth has had anything like this before," continued the nurse, "but I would speculate that since Betsy's skin on her hands and on the bottoms of her feet has not yet reacted, these areas, and probably only these areas, coming into contact with anything wouldn't make her react."

"What will we do while she is still too young to use the potty or toilet?" Megan asked.

"Look for cues," explained the nurse. "Believe it or not, some parents raise their babies without the aid of diapers. These sorts of parents look for cues from their baby when their baby has something to eliminate. If Betsy holds up her hand, or looks you in the face for an extended period of time, take her to the potty right away."

"What about her learning to use the toilet?" Megan asked.

"You'll have to sit her on the toilet in a way that only her hands and feet touch the seat," explained the nurse.

"Can we use soap to get her clean?" Carl asked.

"There are some natural remedy soaps that are very soft on the skin," replied the nurse. "Most of their ingredients are not much different from the body's chemistry, so they should be safe. You can dilute it in water to minimize the risk of a reaction. Then, bathe her again in plain water to wash any soap residue off. If she ever reacts to the soap, stop using it right away, and wash her with water only. It's better that she's only partly clean than she is fatally ill. Do you have a fireplace in your house?"

"We do," Carl replied. "It really helps us feel warm in the winter."

"At the end of every bath, perhaps you could light your fireplace and let her dry off in the living room. Any method of air drying will be all right for Betsy, but the warmer the method, the more Betsy will appreciate it. However, do not use a blow dryer on her, at least in her baby and toddler years, as the loud noise and harsh gust of air could scare her."

Carl spoke up again. "And speaking of 'not much different from the body's chemistry' will she be able to tolerate other peoples' skin? Other human skin will be hardly different from her own, and we would at least like to be able to hold and hug our daughter. Megan will still need to breastfeed her."

"I'm pretty well certain she won't have any reactions to other peoples' skin," the nurse replied. "You just won't be able to have any clothes on the areas where you touch or hold her. While she's a baby, it will be easy for you two to pick her up and hold her as long as you're simply shirtless."

"And toilet paper?" asked Megan. "How can we clean her up after she poops?"

"We'll just have to connect a hose from the sink and spray her clean over the toilet," Carl replied. "We can also make a spray-bottle of the diluted soap solution, that the nurse just recommended, for good measure, and spray some of that on her before we hose her off."

"What about going to bed?" asked Megan.

Another moment of silence followed with the parents, and nurse, completely baffled as to what to do. At the end of all this time, nurse Sheila spoke up once more.

"If you can give Betsy something soft to lie on, something that she wouldn't react to, you would be able to give her a place to sleep. I have heard that silicon is quite versatile. I have a friend called Ellen who makes and sells silicon placemats and picnic cloths. I could contact her and ask if she can make a water mattress out of silicon, and a silicon sheet over top of it. It's not perfect, and I cannot guarantee it will work, but in this case, nothing is going to be perfect. I will be in contact with her first thing when my shift for tonight ends. Then, I'm pretty sure Betsy's bed will be ready by the time she's better enough to leave the hospital. What do you think Megan?"

"Oh Sheila," she sighed. "I think, given the circumstances, it's a brilliant idea. Perhaps even the best or only idea. We will implement it first thing when we get home."

Betsy's condition steadily improved, and she made it through the incident alive and well, but she had to remain in the hospital for four days.

4 A Happy Bath

At last, the parents and the baby arrived home. Dr. Crown had contacted his associates, and read every article he could find regarding skin rashes, childhood development, and allergic reactions. Alas, he could find nothing, and his colleagues could not match Betsy's case with any other. With those findings, Dr. Crown concluded that there was, indeed, no instance of an allergy anywhere in the world, or in history, that resembled Betsy's. Dr. Crown had invented what he felt was the best-fitting name for Betsy's condition: eosinophilic externitis.

As requested, nurse Sheila's friend, Ellen, had made a waterbed for Betsy out of silicon. When Carl and Megan had brought Betsy home from the hospital, they made a side trip to pick up Betsy's bed, and buy a potty as well. Upon arriving home, the first thing Carl and Megan did was put Betsy down on the bed. She sprawled herself out on her new mattress as though it was the most comfortable invention in the world. What pleased Carl and Megan even more was that Betsy's skin seemed to be okay with this substance.

“There has to be some way,” Carl explained to his wife. “I can't think of it at the moment, but there has to be something we can do, so that Betsy doesn't have to live her life entirely alone.”

“Like what?” Megan asked.

Carl spent a minute thinking. Both parents had come from rather large families. Megan was the youngest of three children, with an older sister and older brother, with the brother as the middle child. Carl was the oldest of five children, and had four younger sisters, making him the only boy. However, Carl, Megan and Betsy did not live anywhere near their immediate family anymore, due to how their education and jobs had played out. “Maybe the neighbors will be understanding enough to let Betsy come over once in a while. They live next door to us after all; they might start feeling sympathetic enough to Betsy to have her over. Also, we can always have another child. Even if Betsy can't have any friends, she will at least be able to have a sibling."

"Yeah, I suppose," Megan replied. "We will give that matter some consideration."

Carl opened the box he had just purchased.

"I'll fill Betsy's washing basin while you're setting that up," Megan explained. "Then, we'll put Betsy in the water to stretch herself out. It will be good for her, and she'll like it."

"She'll need to sit down sometimes too," stated Carl. "Betsy won't want to stand, or kneel, all the time, and it won't be good for her muscles. Even if it's just to eat meals, she'll have to sit at some point."

"We can have a silicon pad designed for her to sit on, as well as the waterbed we've designed for her," Megan replied.

Carl continued thinking for a moment. "If she sleeps in a silicon bed, maybe we could have clothes designed for Betsy made out of silicon."

Megan shook her head. "There would be no point, dear. Clothes made of silicon would be transparent, rendering them useless. We couldn't put a dye in them either, to make them opaque, because Betsy would probably be allergic to it. Besides, silicon would not make practical clothing material. It would be very difficult and awkward for her to walk and move around."

However, Carl persisted on considering the situation. "What we could do," he suggested after further thought, "would be to have silicon clothing designed to cover just her waist and chest like a bathing suit, and glue cloth onto the silicon. It won't be proper clothing, but at least she'll be wearing something, and it shouldn't restrict her movement. It would look odd, but it would be better than nothing."

Megan gave Carl's suggestion a moment's thought. "Perhaps," she replied. "That doesn't sound like too bad a suggestion, given the situation. Actually, I think it might work. We'll suggest that to Ellen and have her try it out. For now, I think the best thing for Betsy would be a bath to stretch herself out."

Carl assembled the potty, while Megan stepped into the bathroom. She held Betsy in one arm. With the other, she put Betsy's washing basin below the tap in the bathtub and turned the water on. By the time Carl was finished, Megan had filled the basin with water.

"Now let's see how our baby likes this," Carl smiled.

Megan lowered Betsy into the water, and she immediately giggled and smiled. She stretched her legs out and waved her arms in the water.

Carl and Megan gazed at Betsy in awe and admiration; their baby, happy at last, at total ease and comfort, splashing in the water. Her eyes were sparkling and the tip of her tongue was extending out of her smiling mouth.

"You stay there," Carl grinned. "I'll go get the camera."

He dashed out of the kitchen, fetched his camera from the bedroom, returned, and took a picture.

"This will be the most wonderful picture in my life," cried Carl, a smile spreading all the way across his face. "We will both treasure it forever."

At the end of Betsy's bath, Carl and Megan lit the fireplace, and carried Betsy into the living room. As the fire crackled and Betsy's skin dried, she smiled, and gazed with wide eyes at the fire.

It was a happy day for the Parkers after all.

5 The Love of Christmas

The days turned into weeks; the weeks turned into months, and, before Betsy's parents knew it, their daughter was learning to crawl.

The prospect of crawling made Betsy's parents nervous, as they thought that she would inevitably let her knees touch the floor, which would make her react. However, when Betsy started to crawl, Megan was able to guide Betsy as she crawled so that her knees stayed away from the floor. Betsy's parents dreaded having to take her back to the hospital, but at least her epi-pen was available.

Carl's suggestion of the silicon bathing-suit-like clothing didn't work. The Parkers had "clothes" designed for Betsy in this fashion, but, the moment Carl and Megan dressed Betsy in them, she reacted everywhere on her skin where the silicon was covering her. Her parents had to send her back to the hospital for the afternoon, and Dr. Crown arrived at the conclusion that Betsy's skin had reacted to the silicon because her body yearned to be free of this substance that was trying to bundle it.

That was when Carl and Megan decided that Betsy's situation wasn't salvageable. If they wanted their daughter alive and healthy, she was going to have to live her life never wearing anything, whether they liked it or not, and they weren't going to try anything else, for fear of endangering their child.

"Our daughter is starting to crawl," Carl beamed in awe. "How can any parent not be happy with that?"

"Soon, she'll be walking," smiled Megan. "I can just feel it; it might even be by her first Christmas."

Betsy crawled briskly, around the couch, with her parents following closely behind her, and she was making happy babbling noises all the while. For the past few months, she was making these noises more frequently, and they were becoming more sophisticated.

"I wouldn't be surprised if she starts talking soon," Carl smiled. "That would be lovely. I wonder what her first word will be."

"Probably 'mommy' or 'daddy' or something to that effect," Megan replied.

Soon, the Christmas season was approaching. Carl and Megan had set up a tree and were taking turns between one parent decorating it and the other watching Betsy. They had fixed a string of green and red lights around the tree, and were now hanging ornaments and tinsel.

Megan was applying the tinsel strand-by-strand in specifically-selected places.

"You know, you can get the job done much faster if you pick up a bigger handful, put the first of the handful somewhere high up on the tree, and let the rest slide down to lower branches," Carl advised.

"You can do it your way, I'll do it mine," his wife answered.

Then, Carl thought of something a bit more productive to suggest.

"Hey Megan, what would you say if I suggested that we invite the Nelsons over for Christmas dinner?"

The Nelsons were the Parkers' next-door neighbors. They did not have any children, but they were a happy, friendly young couple. Once every few months, the Parkers and the Nelsons had enjoyed talking together, visiting each other, and inviting each other over for tea, cookies and simple parties. The Nelsons had thrown the Parkers a baby shower when Betsy was born.

"I would say that's a wonderful idea," Megan smiled. "But what about Betsy? What would they think of seeing her?"

"I think they would understand," Carl explained. "They've

lived right next door to us all the time that Betsy has been alive, and it's not like Betsy has a choice about the way she is. Besides, it's Christmas; both Betsy and ourselves could use a bit of company, even if it's for a simple Christmas dinner."

"I think you have a point there," Megan smiled. "You watch Betsy; I'll go knock on their door."

Megan donned her winter coat, opened the door and stepped outside. She turned right at the end of the driveway, walked one house down and knocked on the Nelsons' door.

When the door opened, Megan was delighted to find Anna and Frank Nelson standing inside.

"Merry Christmas Megan," beamed Anna Nelson. "How is life treating you? How is Betsy?"

"Merry Christmas, Anna and Frank. Our family is great, and Betsy is superb," Megan smiled back. Megan wasn't even sure, herself, whether or not she was telling the truth. "I was just wondering," Megan continued, "if maybe, perhaps, you would be interested in coming over for Christmas dinner. I know it's short notice, but we had never thought of asking before today, and probably wouldn't have dared to even if we had."

"Megan, what's wrong?" Anna asked, in a curious, somewhat concerned voice. "Of course we would be honored to come over for Christmas dinner, but something is obviously troubling you. What is it?"

"It's Betsy," Megan explained. "When you come to our house, she won't have anything on. Will that bother you?"

"Oh Megan!" Anna cried. "Of course not. She's just a baby, not quite even a year old yet. Most babies and young children love to play around in the buff. I would, however, advise that you have a diaper on her, at least some of the time, just to protect your carpet, but other than that, there's no problem whatsoever."

Megan struggled with herself. She was finding that telling the truth took more courage than she had thought.

“Betsy can't wear clothes,” Megan told her at last. “She can't wear clothes of any kind, at any time, anywhere on her. When she was nine months old, she had an allergic reaction so horrible, it almost cost her her life. An ambulance rushed her to the hospital, where the doctor confirmed that Betsy has a unique condition that he has termed 'eosinophilic externitis.' Except for her hands, feet and mouth, her skin can't tolerate anything besides water, a special soap we use to wash her, silicon which we use for her bed, and other peoples' skin. She can't brush against anything, and she can't wear clothing, even if it's made of silicon. Ever since that horrific night, we have been terrified that Betsy will make one stumble that could send her back to the hospital.”

At this announcement, Anna and Frank stood there stunned. Finally, Frank cried, “Wow! I had no idea! Thank you for telling us that. Of course we will be willing to come over tomorrow. Betsy could use some company.”

“I only wish she could live a happy life,” Megan sighed.

“You might want to consider contacting the news,” Anna advised. “If Betsy's situation becomes more well-known, hopefully other people will feel compassion for her, and try, in some way, to help her.”

“And what would they do? We want our privacy. We don't want to be in the centre of a gazillion strangers nosing their way into this. We'd never get to have peace and quiet again.”

Mr. and Mrs. Nelson stood in thought for a moment. “Well, you can think about it for a while, and see where the path of Betsy's life takes you. We will come to your house for Christmas dinner,” Anna reassured Megan. “I think it would actually be good both for Betsy, and for you and Carl as well.”

***

On the evening of Christmas Eve, the Parkers hung up three stockings: one for Carl, one for Megan and one for Betsy. Then, they gave Betsy her bedtime wash, and settled her to sleep in her silicon waterbed.

On Christmas morning, the Parkers awoke, happy and eager to celebrate what they had come to view as their favorite holiday. They brought Betsy into the living room where the stockings were full and presents were waiting under the tree.

Carl had received a world atlas and a pair of new glasses; Megan had a white-pearl neckless and a box of fudge; Betsy had an ABC block and miniature teddy bear.

***

That evening, at around five o'clock, there was a knock on the door. Mr. Parker stopped his work on preparing the turkey, stepped out of the kitchen, and answered the door.

Outside were Mr. and Mrs. Nelson.

"Well come on in!" Carl Parker cried, welcoming Frank Nelson with a hug. "We've got the turkey in the oven and I have some mashed potatoes, gravy, stuffing and yams prepared."

"Well we can't wait to taste them!" Mrs. Nelson smiled.

At that moment, Betsy raced forward, in her hobbling crawl, to the top of the staircase, with Megan in her wake.

"And that must be little Betsy," Anna beamed. "She's a beautiful baby."

"I'm so glad you appreciate her," Megan smiled. "Your presence is very welcome. Please remove your shoes and come inside."

The Nelsons removed their shoes and climbed the stairs into the living room. Then, the Nelsons and Mr. Parker sat on the couch, while Mrs. Parker guided Betsy's crawl.

As Betsy came crawling past once again, Mr. and Mrs. Nelson smiled and looked up at Betsy's parents.

"You must be really proud of her," Frank grinned. "She's so happy and carefree, and she's developing such sophisticated movement skills for her age."

"Isn't she?" Megan grinned back. "She's a lot of work, but a lot of fun. We can't wait to see how she develops throughout the various stages of her life."

Soon, it was time to eat dinner. The Parkers had the turkey cut up, with the mashed potatoes on a large plate, and the gravy in a boat. The yams were on a smaller plate. Mr. and Mrs. Parker had prepared a plate of mashed, sweet potatoes for Betsy.

In addition to having a waterbed made out of silicon for Betsy, Carl and Megan had asked Ellen to make a silicon pad so that Betsy could have something to sit down on.

Just before Megan could place Betsy on her silicon pad, Betsy did something that nobody had ever seen her do before.

All on her own, she flexed her back, made her hands let go of the floor, and rose to a standing position.

Everyone, Parkers and Nelsons alike, looked on in amazement and cheered.

"Way to go, Betsy!" Mrs. Parker cried. "Look at you. You're standing all on your own!"

Betsy laughed a happy, playful baby's laugh. With her new-found confidence, she walked a few steps.

"This is wonderful," Megan cried. "You're learning to walk, Betsy. Way to go!"

"Is this her very first?" asked Mrs. Nelson. "Has Betsy ever walked before?"

"She has never walked before," Megan smiled. "This is Betsy's very first. Betsy, I am so proud of you. I love you."

Once again, Betsy smiled at her parents. Then, she turned to the Nelsons and kept right on smiling, a warm, sweet, innocent, playful, loving smile. She made her little baby laugh once again.

"L-lo-ove," Betsy said carefully, spelling every sound of the word out to make sure she said it right.

"What's that you say?" beamed Mrs. Nelson, turning to the baby.

"Love," smiled Betsy again, this time with a little giggle in her voice, and a little more quickly and confidently than before.

"Betsy!" cried her mother, delighted and amazed.

"Your first word!" beamed her father, "And it's 'love' and on Christmas day too. Oh Betsy, we can't express how proud we are."

"She's adorable," Mrs. Nelson smiled. "Thank you, so much, for having us come over."

Betsy turned herself towards her seat and took a few more hobbling steps. Megan picked Betsy up, put her in her seat, and started serving Betsy her potatoes.

It was the happiest Christmas the Parkers and the Nelsons had ever had.

6 Backyard Freedom and a Second Blessing

It wasn't until one summer, a couple of years later, when Carl and Megan started to make plans to build a tall fence around their back yard. Betsy was now two-and-a-half years old, could walk easily, run a little, and had a wonderful crop of light blonde hair that reached to the bottom of her neck.

Her parents had followed through with their plans to give Betsy a sibling, so that Betsy could have at least one kid around to keep her company and to play with. Megan was currently two months pregnant with child number two. However, she was already having misgivings.

"It might be like Betsy," Megan sighed. "We might get another child who can't wear any clothing and has to be put to sleep in a silicon waterbed."

"Calm down, sweetheart," Carl reassured her. "There's no one else on Earth who is like Betsy. She is a miracle, an anomaly. I'll bet anything that the odds of getting another child like her are astronomical; more unlikely than winning millions in the lottery. I am willing to promise you that our next child is going to be fine."

"And even if he or she is fine," Megan insisted. "Think about what we are doing to our second child. How embarrassing it's going to be for him or her to be growing up in a household with Betsy, our naked Betsy, around all the time. Oh, the taunting, the discomfort, the awkwardness there's going to be for our second child. I can just feel it. This wasn't a good idea. I shouldn't have agreed to have another baby."

"Yeah, I see," Carl admitted. "But we have to think about this situation from Betsy's point of view too. We can't have her going through her life never meeting any other children and never making any friends. Everyone faces awkwardness and sometimes embarrassment in life."

"I agree," replied Megan, in a voice understanding to her husband. "I agreed to conceive this baby, and now it's my job to follow through with it, even if it doesn't work out. We are giving Betsy a chance at life. We must give our second baby a chance too."

At around noon that day, Carl drove to the hardware store to purchase some fencing, while Megan stayed at home to watch Betsy. Betsy had been outdoors before. The previous summer, Carl and Megan had figured that, with Betsy being so little, the neighborhood surely wouldn't be bothered by Betsy innocently playing around from time to time. However, during Betsy's third outing, some neighbors from across the street showed up and threatened to call the police unless Carl and Megan put something on Betsy. From then on, Betsy's parents agreed that a fence was essential. They had also nailed up a long wooden plank to the bottom of the living room window, big enough for Betsy to always have the freedom of the living room, even when she would be a bigger girl.

A shopping assistant helped Carl select the tallest, most elegantly-shaped fence. It was rainbow-colored and the top was a beautiful wave pattern. Upon seeing Carl, the cashier told him, "Hey, I know you. You're Carl Parker. You can have that fence for free."

"What? Really?" he cried. He couldn't believe his ears. Could the cashier know about Betsy, and why Carl was buying the fence? Carl couldn't think how the cashier could know about Betsy. The Parkers hadn't told anyone. At the same time, Carl couldn't think of any other reason why the cashier would give Carl the fencing free of charge. Oh well, it was a free deal no matter what. Carl smiled back and said, "Thank you. I will let my wife know when I get home."

When Carl arrived home, he busied himself putting the fence

up all around the back yard.

"Soon, Betsy will have somewhere to play," he smiled to his wife. "You know, the clerk gave me this fence for free. I have a feeling he knows about Betsy. I'm starting to think we should get her story out into the open, let the news know. Keeping it a secret is only hiding Betsy away all the more, and making us look like we're ashamed of our own child."

Megan thought about it for a minute. "I think I agree with you dear," she replied at last, "but I would give it a little more time. Wait until Betsy is old enough to understand what it's about. Also, I wouldn't want them broadcasting her on television. There would be a world full of strangers seeing her, and some would exploit it."

"If they show Betsy, they wouldn't show her whole body," explained Carl. "They would just show her face, at most, and that is all they would need to show. There's no need for us to be on television either. Our story can be in the paper."

By four o'clock that afternoon, Carl had finished putting up the fence. "Hey Betsy!" he called, "You want to come out and play?"

Carl opened the door to the back yard and Betsy came trotting out. "Yes! Yes!" she smiled, with a giggle in her voice. "I love to play!" She ran outside in a playful trot, clapping her hands.

Betsy ran across the yard, and came to a stop at the edge of her splash pool. Carl took her hands, picked her up and put her in the water. The second Betsy was in the water, she began splashing about.

"It's so lovely to see Betsy splashing, playing, and being so happy," Carl grinned, turning to Megan.

"That it is, dear," she smiled back.

"In seven more months, Betsy will have a new brother or sister to keep her company. That will really be wonderful. Say, what do you think our new baby is going to be? Girl or boy?"

"I'm not too sure with this one," Megan replied, "but I guess 'not too sure' is a different feeling from 'definitely a girl' like I felt when I was carrying Betsy. I've heard that mothers who are carrying the opposite sex from a previous pregnancy often feel different from how they felt during that previous pregnancy, so I'm guessing it's going to be a boy."

"Well, that's a good guess, and some good logic there. We should think hard about boy names and girl names both though. You picked out 'Betsy' before she was born because you felt sure it would be a girl, but you just got lucky. You don't want to settle your mind that this one is going to be a boy, pick out a boy's name, and find it's another girl."

"I guess not," Megan replied.

"Hey, me Bessie! Bessie!" Betsy cried from her play bath.

"That's right, my darling," Megan beamed, "You're Betsy. We're talking about you."

Twenty minutes later, Betsy had had enough of her splash pool. She held out her hands, and Carl picked her out. He went inside to prepare some lemonade. Soon, he was back with a pitcher and some plastic cups.

"Oh, that looks wonderful dear!" Megan cried. "Thank you so much!"

"Thank you," Betsy mouthed after her mother.

After they had started drinking their lemonade, a fly fell into Betsy's drink. It started scrambling on the surface of the liquid to keep from drowning.

Betsy looked at it, gently dipped her finger into her drink, and pulled the fly out, "Don't dwown, fly," she said, in a comforting, kind of endearing voice. She didn't show the slightest hint of adversity about the insect, nor a trace of hard feelings towards it for falling in. She gazed, with a happy and loving face at the fly, while it was still on her finger, pleased with herself that she had just saved this little bug's life. The fly flew away, and Betsy continued to gaze after it in awe, as it flew into the distance and out of sight.

After the Parkers had finished their drinks, Betsy proceeded, once more, to run around on the lawn. She ran around and around the perimeter of the back yard in circles many times. At one point, Betsy jumped. "Hey, my bum wiggles!" she called out. She jumped again, felt her buttocks jiggle once more, and made another strong, joyous, giggling laugh. Then, she jumped up and down again and again, many times, as her bum wiggled and jiggled all the while, with Betsy laughing and giggling the whole time.

Carl watched his daughter and laughed.

The summer wore on, and Betsy had many more fun outings in her back yard that she had come to adore like a paradise. While Betsy was inside, she occupied herself with solving simple children's puzzles, and playing with toys. When the fall arrived and the weather became too cool for Betsy to play outside anymore, her parents could tell that Betsy missed the back yard and would have to endure all of fall, winter and spring before she could see it again.

"Oh, don't worry about Betsy," Carl commented to his wife. "I know she misses going outside, but she has so much fun in the house as well. She is making such progress with her hands and with her vocabulary."

Carl and Megan had kept Betsy's crib so that a future baby could use it. They also planned to let the new baby have Betsy's clothes that Carl and Megan had bought for Betsy when she was a newborn baby.

Before the Parkers knew it, it was February, and the day was approaching when Megan's baby was due. Megan turned to Carl and asked him, "I can feel my baby coming. Could you please nip over to the Nelsons and ask them to come and babysit Betsy like we arranged?"

Carl put on his coat and shoes and headed next door. When he knocked, Anna and Frank answered as though they had been waiting for him.

"Megan is just about to have her second baby," Mr. Parker explained. "Can you come and babysit Betsy?"

"Of course! We'd be happy to," smiled Mrs. Nelson. "Congratulations on Megan having her second baby and I hope everything goes well."

The Nelsons came to babysit Betsy, and Carl drove Megan to the hospital once again.

Later that evening, on February 17, the baby was born.

"Congratulations Megan!" nurse Ken Reynolds beamed. "You have another little girl!"

"Laura," breathed Megan, smiling at her baby.

7 The Teaching Begins

Betsy was delighted when her parents brought Laura home from the hospital.

“Look Betsy,” Megan smiled at her. “You have a baby sister.”

Betsy put down her book 'The Teddy Bears' Picnic' and ran to the top of the stairs to see her new sister.

“A sisser, a sisser!” exclaimed Betsy, her eyes wide, and a smile splitting her face.

“Her name is 'Laura,'” explained her mother. “Can you say 'Laura' Betsy?”

“Lo-wa, Lo-wa,” smiled Betsy.

Her parents smiled and laughed.

There were never any abnormalities with Laura Elizabeth Parker. She made it through one month, then two months, then three months with no skin reactions, no food reactions, or any kind of adverse reactions at all. She was normal in every conceivable way, and beautiful and healthy as well.

She had a patch of light brown hair, unlike the light blonde that Betsy had. Mr. and Mrs. Parker also noticed that Laura was more moody than Betsy had been as a baby. Laura cried more often and didn't smile quite as much. She still smiled frequently, at her parents, at Betsy, and at various pictures and mobiles around the house, but her parents could detect a solemness in Laura that hadn't been present in Betsy.

By now, it was the middle of May, and the weather was just getting warm enough for Betsy to get out into the back yard once again. Her parents decided it would be good for Laura to get out too. Laura was dressed in a butterfly diaper and a purple and pink striped jumper.

Betsy was delighted. She cried with joy and ran towards Laura, waving her hands in the air, as her parents were about to head out the door. "You coming Low-ra?" Betsy called. "You'll love it, and I don't want to be the only kid out here!"

Carl and Megan were elated at how well Betsy was getting along with Laura. Even with Laura being a baby, and Betsy being her three-year-old big sister, it couldn't be plainer that Betsy adored Laura and was always looking out for her. It was as if Betsy had made her very first friend.

Megan unfolded a towel from the linen closet, set it on the grass and put Laura down on the towel.

Once Laura was on the towel, she gazed with wide, curious eyes at the grassy lawn. A cricket hopped past and Laura extended her hand to try to feel it. However, the cricket hopped away before the baby could reach it. A hint of a puzzled, disappointed expression crossed Laura's face.

There were still several cool or rainy days ahead before summer started properly. As often as Betsy and Laura's parents could, they brought their daughters onto the lawn. Betsy sometimes played. Other times, she admired her sister. Laura always lay on her blanket looking around the lawn.

Carl turned to Megan, "You know dear," he explained. "Starting this September, I really think it's time we started homeschooling Betsy. She would be starting preschool this coming year, and she needs an education, one way or another."

"I agree dear," Megan replied. "I have been thinking the same thing. I also think that now is the time to call the press about Betsy. It is time to get our story out. We keep talking about doing this but we never actually do anything. I think it's time that we really do something. We can't keep Betsy surrounded in a shell of ignorance from the rest of the world. Already, people around our neighborhood are asking why they never see Betsy. It's humiliating."

Even after that conversation, Carl and Megan still did not act on Megan's request right away. However, as the summer wore on, Betsy's parents were beginning to notice a subtle quietness about Betsy, suggesting to them that it was starting to dawn on Betsy that she was different. Betsy was still a happy, playful girl, and her parents believed that anyone outside the family would not yet be able to notice the change.

Eventually, it was the middle of August and, especially with school resuming in a couple of weeks, Carl and Megan decided that now was the day to contact the newspaper, before they put it off one more day, then another, then another, like they had been doing, and perpetuating the vicious circle of talking about it and never doing it.

Carl picked up the phone and dialled the news station's number. He was nervous about the reaction he would get (The girl who couldn't wear clothes?). Would the news people think he was insane, or that he was trying to be funny?

"Hello there," came a man's voice from the other end.

The time was now. Carl took a couple of deep breaths, made his muscles relax, and breathed. "Hello, my name is Carl Parker. I am thirty-six years old and married to Megan Parker, formerly Willow, and I am calling to report that we have a very unusual daughter that I feel the press ought to know about."

"Unusual?" asked the voice. "How?"

"Well ... she was born normal and healthy; six weeks later, she had an allergic reaction to her diaper and we had to take her to the hospital. Then she had a much more severe reaction several months later. She's a wonderful, charming little girl; she really is. She smiles a lot, loves nature, loves her new sister; she ..."

"Sir, you're stalling. Please tell me what's unusual about her."

Carl took another deep breath and mustered his courage once

more. At that point, he noticed that he had never told the news man his daughter's name.

"Her name is Betsy," Carl explained. "She is three-and-a-half years old, and she's ..."

He was feeling really stupid and silly now. He drew another breath, formed the words in his mouth and blurted out, "She-has-a-life-threatening-allergic-condition-that-prevents-her-from-wearing-any-clothes."

Then, Carl exhaled fast and deeply out his mouth.

After this announcement, there was a minute of silence.

"Sir," asked the man on the phone at the end of the long pause. "Are you okay?"

"I'm okay," he assured the news man, "and so is my wife. We've been wanting to let the news know for a long time now, but we've never actually gotten around to doing it."

"Have you had your mental health assessed?"

This question cut Carl to the quick. "I don't need my mental health assessed!" he cried. "Even the doctor at the hospital contends that my wife and I are both sane, loving parents. Dr. Derek Crown confirmed that this is what is wrong with Betsy. He let us keep his business card. If you want proof that I am not lying, and not insane, you can call him yourself."

"I will have to call him," the man's voice continued. "Every time there is a medical case reported in a newspaper, the journalist must consult any doctors involved; both to obtain consent to disclose medical information, and to obtain a reliable source to ensure the story is not a hoax. My name is Smith Charles, by the way. If you ever want me over the phone again in the future, my extension is 2 at the end of the news station's regular phone number."

"So you will put it in the paper?"

"After I have consulted your doctor, yes," Smith replied. "If what you say about your daughter is true, a news story will give the public a chance to know about your daughter, and, hopefully give her at least a bit of compassion."

"Will my family and I be coming to the news station, or will you be coming here?"

"Well, I don't see how you're going to transport your daughter if she's got no clothes on. We will come to your house to do a quick interview, and take a few pictures. Please have your daughter stand behind a couch or something so that we don't see all of her. Where do you live?"

"9635 82 Street."

"We're thinking that we will bring Dr. Crown with us to take part in the interview if he's available," explained Smith. "Would that be all right with you?"

"Yes, yes, of course it would."

"Good, well I had better be going now. See you in about an hour."

"Goodbye, Smith Charles," and the two men hung up.

"How did it go?" Megan asked her husband after Carl had hung up. "Is there going to be a news story?"

"Yes, there is," Carl smiled. "The news guy was really shocked for a bit, and couldn't believe I was telling the truth. But I managed to convince him that this is real, and they'll be over in about an hour."

"Oh, that's wonderful," Megan smiled.

An hour later, there was a knock at the door. Megan got up from the couch to answer it, as Betsy came hurrying to the door, "Who is it?" she cried. "Is that the Nelsons?"

The people on the other side of the door saw Betsy running up, just as Megan was opening it. They all smiled and laughed at this cute, pleasing sight, as the child ran down the stairs and onto the landing.

The crew at the other side of the door consisted of a total of three people. One was the news man Smith Charles (he had his name pinned onto his shirt), another was a woman, tagged as 'Martha Lawrence,' apparently a partner or co-worker of Smith Charles, and the third was Dr. Derek Crown from the hospital.

"It's such a pleasure to see Betsy so happy, healthy and growing so well," smiled Dr. Crown. "She seems eager to meet us too."

"She is," Carl smiled back. "We have two daughters now, by the way. Laura was born just last February. There is nothing unusual about Laura."

"Oh, that's wonderful," smiled the doctor.

"Please," Carl smiled. "Feel free to remove your shoes and come on in."

The three guests removed their shoes and made their way up the stairs, into the living room. The two news people started setting up their equipment.

When the camera was ready, Smith Charles directed Betsy to stand behind the couch.

"But why?" Betsy asked, in a voice that indicated she knew she was being told to hide herself, but she obeyed.

"You'll have to respect Betsy," Carl explained, hurt that his own daughter was now, verbally, being treated as though merely being in this world was unacceptable. "She has never been told to stand out of sight of anyone before."

All the same, the news people positioned the Parkers in a way they felt was the most picturesque. They had Carl stand on the left side of the couch, Megan stand on the right side, and had them put Laura, who was in her cuddle-seat, down on the couch in front of Megan. The end result was Carl and Megan in full view, Laura visible on the couch, with only Betsy's face poking out from behind.

"So, please describe your daughter's medical condition in as much detail as you possibly can," said Smith.

Carl and Megan, together, told Smith the complete story from Betsy's birth, her first rash, their finding that practically nothing could touch her skin, the doctor's reaction, and how they had come to cope with the situation and the difficulties surrounding it all these years. Part way through, they had Dr. Crown come to the front and join the family, and he explained how it was unquestionable that this was, indeed, what was wrong with Betsy, and how, for once in his career, he had been unable to tell the parents what to do.

"Betsy?" asked Martha, when all this was over. "What do you like to do?"

"I like to weed pick-tue books, I like back yard, I like to dwaw, I like my toys, I like my animals, I love my sister Laura."

"That's wonderful," beamed Martha.

She bent down to the tripod that they had set up, and took a picture, with the family still standing in the same position in which they been when the news crew first made their set-up.

"And how is your younger daughter, Laura?" asked Smith.

Once again the parents, in turn, told the news crew of how they'd had another child so that Betsy would have at least one other kid to play with, that Laura had shown curiosity about her surroundings on the lawn, including the cricket that had hopped across the grass, and how she had not yet been sick in any way.

At the end of all this, Martha spoke up once more. "Anything more you would like to add?"

Carl and Megan thought for a moment. Then Carl said, "No, I think that will be everything."

"Then let me take one more picture, just before we leave," smiled Martha. "Say 'cheese' everybody. One, two..."

"THREE!!!" Betsy cried, and ran out from behind the couch. Before Martha could stop herself, the camera flashed, and the entirety of Betsy was caught in the picture.

Carl and Megan burst into peals of laughter. "Wow, that should help get the message out about the kind of girl Betsy is," Carl commented.

But the news crew were not laughing. "We'll have to retake the picture, this time having Betsy standing behind the couch," Martha explained. "Either that, or not take it at all. We can't put pictures like that one in the newspaper."

Not only did Martha insist on not publishing that last picture, she proceeded to open her camera, pull the roll of film out and throw it in the garbage. She opened her purse, picked a new roll out, and put it in her camera. "Do you want a picture?" she asked.

Realizing that Martha had just thrown away the first picture, in which the parents were standing on either side of the couch, with Betsy standing behind, he reluctantly agreed, so that the paper could show at least one picture of the family.

She re-posed them in the way they had been when they took the first picture, told Betsy very firmly to stay put, and took one more picture.

"There," she said. "I think that will be everything. Come on, Smith. We'd better be on our way."

Smith turned to the parents. "Thank you for calling us out," he grinned. "The story should appear in the newspaper within the next few days."

"Bye bye now," Dr. Crown waved.

"Bye!" waved the parents.

"Bye! Bye!" Betsy called.

***

When Betsy's first day of homeschooling arrived, Megan brought an alphabet book into the living room. She opened the cover and showed Betsy the first page. It had a giant 'A' on it.

"That's an 'A' Betsy," Megan smiled. "Can you say 'A'?"

"Yeah! Ai!" the child beamed.

"It makes the 'Ah' sound."

Over the next hour, the mother and daughter worked through the book one letter at a time. After making Betsy say 'Z' Megan took a break, and served Betsy some milk and cookies.

As Betsy was having her fill, Carl came up the stairs with a newspaper.

"Look dear!" he exclaimed. "We have made headline news!"

"That's wonderful dear," Megan smiled back at him. "Let me look at what it says," and they both read the news story.

Girl Allergic to Clothing and Everything Tangible

3-year-old Betsy Parker has a unique condition. She was born unable to touch anything, anywhere on her skin, except her hands and feet. Betsy lives her whole life in the nude, and has, therefore, been unable to meet any other children.

Her parents, Carl and Megan Parker, are homeschooling their daughter. She has a six-month-old sister Laura, who does not share Betsy's condition, and has never reacted abnormally to any substance.

"We first began to fear for our daughter at around 3am when she was barely nine months old," says father Carl. "She had a reaction so bad, her whole skin was purple and she was vomiting.

We were unsure whether our daughter was going to make it. It was then that it occurred to us that maybe she would never be able to wear any clothes, ever again, and that we would have to separate our daughter from society forever."

It was Dr. Derek Crown of St. Hubert's hospital who later confirmed this to be the case.

"I was in shock," he said. "I didn't know what to tell the parents to do with Betsy. Eventually, I informed them that she would have to be a hermit, who would be homeschooled, and separated from all other kids, but it was horrible ... it was truly, truly horrible."

Dr. Crown, who has termed Betsy's condition 'Eosinophilic Externitis' confirms that the case is unique, in the world and in history, but he doesn't think Betsy will ever get over it. She will have the condition the rest of her life.

Meanwhile, the Parkers are keeping close watch over Betsy and nurturing her, while Betsy goes about her childhood enjoying her back yard, drawing, playing with her toys and animals, and doting on her baby sister. Her parents have sheltered their back yard so that she can play outside, but only time will tell how the rest of her life will unfold.

Above the text was the picture that Martha had taken of the family standing around the couch, with Betsy, showing nothing but her face, peeking out from behind.

"Well," breathed Carl. "Looks like they did a pretty good job. We will see what people think. Hopefully, there will be at least a shred of compassion for Betsy now."

"Me too," sighed Megan. "I better go back to teaching her. I think break time is over."

She led Betsy back into the living room and had a simple puzzle set up for her. It was various dinosaurs (a stegosaurus, a pterodactyl, a brontosaurus, a triceratops, and a T-rex) carved into foam, in which a young child could lift the dinosaur shapes out, and put them back into their moulds.

Betsy, first, picked the whole puzzle up to examine it, and the shapes within it. She put her hands on the triceratops, said 'triceratops' and pushed it out of its frame. Then, she moved her fingers to the pterodactyl, said 'pterodactyl' and did the same. As she pushed every shape out, she said the name of its respective dinosaur.

Soon, all five shapes were out of their frames.

"Very good, Betsy," her mother smiled. "Can you put them back in now?"

The little girl crouched down on the floor, on her feet only, put the empty frame down, and, one by one, she put the dinosaurs back into their frames.

"That's amazing Betsy!" cried her mother. "I am so proud of you!"

8 Betsy Learns the Truth

Over the next few days, the Parkers received several phone calls from people around the neighborhood, and from abroad. Some people who called were comforting, reassuring and understanding. A lot of the people in the neighborhood thanked the Parkers for letting them know about Betsy, and that now they knew why they hadn't been seeing anything of her in all these years.

Other calls were nasty, angry and intimidating, and unfortunately, these sorts of calls were not uncommon. Some even vented that the Parkers had to remove Laura from the home, so that she wouldn't grow up in a household with Betsy, and, unless the Parkers did so now, they wouldn't let their children play with Laura either.

"I find it sad, the prejudice and hatred some kids must be learning," sighed Carl. "I think it's children with parents like these that should be removed from their home."

"I'm afraid I have to agree with you," sighed Megan. "I don't even think they see our Betsy as a human being. It's like she's an alien from outer space that's landed on Earth. It scares them, and they don't know how to react."

"It's history replaying itself," sighed Carl. "There have been many people treated just like that: slaves, blacks, Jews, even women; and now it's our sweet, intelligent, loving daughter."

A few minutes later, the phone rang once again.

"I'll get it," breathed Carl, and stepped towards the phone. "Hello," he said.

"Oh hi," came a happy, welcoming, woman's voice on the other end. "We read about Betsy in the paper. Thank you so much for telling us about your daughter. I was wondering where she had got to. I have a wonderful young son and daughter. If you want, I could bring my kids over to play with Betsy."

"What? Really?" cried Carl amazed. This had to be a dream. Nobody had ever reacted this way to Betsy.

"I understand Betsy must be lonely," the woman continued. "I'm Penny Barnes by the way. I live across the street, on the other end of the road."

"Well Penny," Carl continued. "Thank you so much. I think that would be a great idea, but what would your kids think?"

"I think they'd understand, and they're still young enough to feel comfortable about it. I don't think it's going to hurt them in any way. My son, Kyle, is five, and my daughter, Emma, is three."

"Certainly!" cried Carl. "Betsy would be delighted. Would you be able to bring them over this afternoon?"

"Sure, I'd be able to. How does three to five o'clock sound to you?"

"That would be lovely. See you then."

And they hung up.

Carl was ecstatic! Upon putting the receiver down, he ran to his wife and told her the great news.

"That's wonderful Carl!" cried Megan. "I never thought anyone would be understanding enough towards Betsy to let their kids come over. I really think, all in all, we did the right thing by putting Betsy's situation in the paper."

As the Parkers awaited the arrival of Penny and her children, Carl set up some chips with dip, cookies and crackers in the living room. He vacuumed the house, and straightened the pictures. Then, he and his wife waited eagerly in the living room for the knock on the door.

"You're getting visitors, Betsy," Megan smiled. "The first children, outside of this family, will be coming to play with you shortly."

"I'm getting friends?" cried Betsy jubilantly. "I've never played with other kids before!"

Betsy ran to the top of the stairs, all excited, eagerly awaiting the knock that was about to come. For the next ten minutes, she didn't move. She stood there, in exactly the same place, her little eyes intent on the door.

When the knock finally came, Betsy let out a squeal of delight, hurried down the stairs and pulled the door open.

"Hello there!" cried the woman at the other side. "You must be Betsy Parker."

This woman was accompanied by a man, of similar age, obviously her husband, a little boy, and a little girl.

"I'm Penny Barnes, and this is my husband Jack," she explained, facing Mr. and Mrs. Parker. "Well, children," she smiled, turning to her kids. "Feel free to come in and meet Betsy. She has an allergic skin condition that prevents her from wearing any clothing, but I know she is just like any other girl on the inside."

"Oh boy!" cried Kyle, and ran into the house, without even taking his shoes off.

"Kyle!" called his mother. "Shoes off, please."

"Yes, mom," he sighed. He stepped back down the stairs, and removed his shoes on the landing.

Emma knelt down, and quietly removed her shoes before entering the house.

"Now," smiled Penny. "We will leave you to it. See you at five o'clock."

"Come on," beamed Betsy to the two children. "I will take you to the living room." She stepped back up the stairs, leading the children inside.

She led them to the coffee table, where the treats were set up.

In a minute, Betsy, Kyle and Emma were digging into the chips, cookies and crackers.

"These are delicious!" cried Kyle. "I could eat these every day!"

"Not every day," chuckled Emma, "You need your veggies too. Mommy said so."

"Mommy doesn't know what good food is," smirked Kyle to his sister. "She says it herself 'You don't know it if you don't try it' and I've never seen her try cookies."

After they had had enough of eating treats, the children proceeded to play hide and seek around the house.

Betsy never hid, but she did all the seeking. At one point, Betsy found Emma hidden in the broom closet. Later, Kyle thought it would be clever to hide in the cupboard, but Carl informed him that the cupboard was out of bounds.

Eventually, Betsy and the other children had had enough of hide and seek, and she led them out into the back yard. Betsy stepped over to the corner of the yard, brought out a soccer ball, and the children proceeded to play. They kicked the ball around the back yard and between each other. Betsy and her new friends walked, sometimes ran, around the yard, chasing the ball, so they could kick it somewhere else. Sometimes, one kid would kick it somewhere far away, out on the yard, away from the others, and all three children ran, laughing, after the ball to continue playing with it. All the while, every child watched the ball in case it came to him or her.

Kyle and Emma spent the entire two hours dressed, including the time outdoors, but before either the children or Betsy's parents knew it, there came a knock on the door. It was five o'clock, and Mr. and Mrs. Barnes had arrived. "I'll go get Kyle and Emma," Carl explained.

He stepped towards the back deck, as Penny and Jack

followed.

"Oh, that is beautiful," breathed Carl when he saw the children playing their own version of soccer. "I can't even bear to disturb it. Would you mind if I get a picture? You'd be okay with your children being in it, wouldn't you?"

"Of course," replied Jack.

Carl dashed to his room and got his camera.

He returned to the deck, seconds later, with the camera around his neck. "This is the most innocent thing I have ever seen," Carl beamed. "My daughter, completely naked and at ease, respecting the other children's choice to be clothed, and the other children completely at ease with my daughter the way she is, all three simply playing soccer on the lawn. I envy Betsy; I really do. I wish I could become just like her, and stay that way all the rest of my life."

He pressed the shutter, and the picture was taken.

Penny was the one to disturb this scene. "Kyle, Emma, it's time to go home now!"

The little boy and girl sighed and turned away from the ball.

"That was fun, Betsy," smiled Kyle. "I hope I can come over to your house again."

"See you later!" Betsy called, waving after him.

In a few more minutes, Kyle, Emma and their parents had left.

Betsy's homeschooling was proceeding amazingly well. By the time the regular schools' classes had ended for Christmas Holidays, Betsy could sing the alphabet, and count to ten. She was saying the names of animals and objects in picture books.

"Say, Betsy," Megan smiled. "What do you want for Christmas?"

"A chocolate Santa," grinned Betsy.

"That's all?" asked her mother. "You don't want anything more?"

"Nothing more," Betsy beamed.

"Very well," said Megan, and proceeded to leave the room.

"Oh!" Betsy called, as her mother was almost out. "I know what more I want."

"And what's that?" asked Megan.

"You, daddy, and Laura," Betsy beamed back at her.

"Oh you sweet little thing!" Megan cried, and ran back into the living room, spread her arms wide, and just as she was about to wrap them around Betsy, Megan cried ...

"Oops! So sorry! Forgot for a moment, I can't do that!"

Megan put her arms back to her sides, and with a disappointed expression, left the room.

Betsy watched her mother leave the room. Tears formed in the little girl's eyes, and she began to cry.

Megan, not knowing what to do or say, stepped back into the living room, and cried too. Seeing each other crying reassured both the mother and daughter, and soon, they had got over their feelings of hurt and dried their tears.

"Let's be happy," wept Megan still sniffling a little. "It is just about Christmas after all."

The Christmas season came for Betsy, just as it had the past few years. However, over the past several days, Carl and Megan could feel Betsy's sense of withdrawal, that they had sensed all summer, intensifying. She was growing quieter and quieter, and she was smiling far less often than she used to. She seemed lost in her own world, and confused.

It had gotten to the point where it was no longer subtle, but painful and obvious. Anybody would have been able to see the change by now.

"Should we ask her what's wrong?" Megan asked. "Try to comfort her?"

“No,” replied Carl. “Give her some time; she'll speak out on her own.”

On the morning of Christmas, Betsy looked at the chocolate Santa her parents had given to her, but she showed no interest in eating it. Finally, she looked up at her mother and asked,

“Something's wrong with me, isn't there?”

“Oh Betsy!” her mother cried. “How do you know?”

“I don't go to school. I don't see other kids. You all wear clothes, but I can't.”

When Megan looked at Betsy, she could feel her daughter's sense of loss within herself. Megan proceeded to remove her pants, keeping everything else on, even her underwear, and sat down on the couch.

“Here Betsy,” Megan beamed. “Come sit on my lap.”

Betsy stepped towards her mother, turned around, and sat on her mother's bare lap. It was such a relaxing position, for Betsy, that a smile, a ray of sunlight, broke through the clouds on Betsy's face, and she made another one of her playful laughs.

“Thank you, Mommy,” Betsy smiled. “I like sitting like this.”

But as Betsy relaxed on her mother's lap, her overall mood remained quiet and saddened, so her mother spoke to her once more.

“Betsy Alicia Parker,” her mother breathed happily to her. “You are a wonderful girl; you show a quality of love and compassion I have never seen from anyone else who has come into my life. We are all different, Betsy; every one of us. In all of this world, there are no two people who are the same, and you are a person too, and different; and you know what's best of all? You're my little girl. I love you, I will always love you, and I will love you no matter what other people think of you, no matter what other people say about you, no matter how other people treat you.”

“But you're the only one who says that, you and daddy. Why

don't others like me?"

"You see, Betsy; nobody else on this planet gets the reactions on their skin that you do. Not me, not daddy, not Laura, not the Nelsons, not the Barnes's, nobody. Everybody has to wear clothes, and keep them on at all times. It's the way of human life. Society will expect you to wear clothes too, but you can't, because you're allergic to everything that touches you on the outside. I'm sorry Betsy, but the way you spend your life, always in the house or back yard, is the way you're going to be living all the rest of your life. I wish there was something I could do about it, but I can't."

"What?" cried Betsy ... "Why?"

The voice of Carl echoed from the kitchen. "How many pieces of French toast do you want, girls?" he called, as he stepped into the living room. He had been frying French toast prepared in egg nog.

As soon as he stepped into the living room, he sensed, immediately, that something was wrong.

"Er, what's going on?" Carl asked.

"Betsy's figured out the truth," Megan sighed sadly.

9 The Minister's Visit

In the days that followed the Christmas morning when Betsy found out the truth, her demeanor and mood took a turn for the worse. Betsy no longer smiled, played, or ran around the house. She spent many hours sitting on her silicon waterbed, looking lost and acting quiet, other times taking out, and putting back the dinosaurs in her dinosaur puzzle.

Twenty-two days after Christmas Day, Betsy's fourth birthday arrived, but she was still not herself. She invited Kyle and Emma over to celebrate her birthday with her. Carl and Megan had prepared a vanilla unicorn birthday cake, with a pink icing horn, and yellow icing and white sprinkles for fur. Megan had squeezed a message onto the cake, in red gelatin letters, reading, "Our beautiful daughter is 4. Happy birthday Betsy."

Betsy opened her presents (a sunny island puzzle from Carl, a porcelain unicorn from Megan, a stuffed hedgehog from Kyle, and a box of colorful rocks from Emma), and ate her cake, but even the Barnes's children were noticing that Betsy was more quiet than usual.

"Hey Betsy," Kyle asked, "why are you so quiet? You're always so playful when we come over."

"I can't wear clothes," Betsy replied, "and that's not allowed."

"Who told you that?" Kyle asked back.

"Mommy," Betsy replied. "She says I'm going to spend the rest of my life in the house and back yard."

"Hey, that's not fair," said Emma, "but you can still play with us."

"I don't want to play," Betsy said.

"Maybe this will help," said Emma, and she proceeded to remove all her clothes, until she was in her bare skin.

"Tag! You're it!" Emma cried at Betsy, tagging her on the shoulder.

"Hey! Me too!" Kyle cried. He pulled off all his clothes, dropped then in a heap next to Emma's, and joined in the game.

With a renewed smile, and sense of playfulness, Betsy began to chase after her friends, around the living room, happy that they were now both just as bare as she was. Eventually, Betsy caught up to Emma.

"Tag!" Betsy called, tagging Emma on the shoulder.

Emma let out a squeal and began to chase her brother, to tag him.

"Wow Betsy!" Carl cried, as he stepped into the living room. "You're playing again. This is so wonderful to see."

After Carl said this, Emma tagged her brother, and he began to chase after Betsy.

"Daddy! Kyle is chasing me!" Betsy cried in a laugh, as her friend ran after her to tag her once again.

After the cake, the presents, and the game of tag, Mr. and Mrs. Barnes arrived to pick their children up. Kyle and Emma put their clothes back on, and left for the evening.

"Thank you for having us over," Kyle smiled at Betsy. "When you're sad, don't forget that you have us."

"Good night, Betsy. Happy birthday," Emma waved, as she and her brother headed out the door, towards their parents' car.

"Happy birthday!" Betsy called back.

Kyle and Emma burst into fits of laughter.

"Wow Betsy!" chuckled Jack Barnes, laughing too. "It's not *Emma's* birthday."

Carl and Megan were relieved that Betsy was happy once again, but, to their disappointment, it was a short-lived happiness. Later that evening, after the Barnes's children had left, Betsy became quiet again, and she still hadn't eaten her chocolate Santa from Christmas.

"There has to be something we can do about this," said Megan, turning to Carl. "Should we get a doctor to come over?"

Carl spent a few minutes thinking. Then, a light came on in his face. "I've got an even better idea," he suggested. "How about we invite our minister, Reverend Ben Herb, over. With Betsy being more aware of the world, and having learned that others will have a hard time accepting her for who she is, I think that the time has come for a proper adult authority figure to come to our house who will accept her, with unconditional love, as one of God's children."

"That's a wonderful idea," Megan smiled. "I think that will do Betsy some good, and give her hope."

Carl thumbed through the phonebook until he came to Herb, Reverend Ben. Then, he dialled his number.

Unlike Carl's phone conversation with the news man, Carl's conversation with Ben Herb was smooth and confident from the beginning. Ben Herb had read Betsy's story in the paper, and he had wanted to help her. Since Ben had learned of Betsy's situation, he had engaged in a discussion with his elders, and they had come to an agreement that it would be in Betsy's and God's best interests that Ben helped Betsy. Ben agreed to come over that evening, just before Betsy's bedtime.

"Hey Betsy," Carl smiled after he had hung up the phone. "Minister Ben Herb is coming over."

"What's a mimister?" Betsy asked.

"A servant of God," Carl explained. "Someone who guides us in our lives, and helps us become more connected with God."

"Who's God?" Betsy asked.

Carl looked pensive, then smiled. "Ben Herb will tell you," he replied.

Half an hour later, a knock sounded. Betsy hurried down the stairs and pulled the door open, as Carl followed.

"Hello Ben," Carl smiled. "Come on in. Take a seat in the living room."

"Hi there, Betsy," Ben smiled. "You are growing so nicely. I am so proud."

As Ben removed his shoes, Laura came crawling down the hallway, past the top of the staircase, with Megan right behind her, guiding her second daughter's crawl.

"And that must be little Laura," continued the minister, his smile growing. "Looks like she's coming along too."

"She is," smiled Megan.

"La la," said Laura, as she crawled into the living room, around the couch.

After the minister's shoes were off, Betsy called, "Come in!" and she headed up the stairs, leading the minister inside.

Once everyone was seated in the living room (Betsy on her silicon pad on the couch) Carl began to tell the minister about Betsy.

"She was so full of beans in her early life," Carl began. "She loved to smile, run, laugh, and play in the back yard. I wish you could hear how she used to laugh."

"Well, she sounds like quite the character," smiled the minister. "Hey Betsy," Ben continued, turning to the girl. "Come here; I want to tell you a story."

"You do?" Betsy beamed. "I love stories."

Betsy stood up from the couch, and moved her pad to the carpet, where she knelt down on the floor in front of the minister.

"One day," began the minister, "a swarm of bright spiritual attributions, energy, and particles too small for the human eye to see accumulated together. When they met, they arranged themselves to form a little, human, girl. God was the supreme being who had arranged for all of this to happen. God had plans for this little girl to guard his kingdom, to keep his kingdom in order, to make peace in his kingdom, and to be one piece in a great puzzle in restoring his kingdom to paradise. Without that one piece in the puzzle, the kingdom of God would be incomplete."

"What picture is the puzzle when it's finished?" Betsy asked.

"A picture of perfect peace, friendship, and harmony," Ben replied, "but that picture has yet to be finished because some pieces are missing; some pieces have yet to find their place in the puzzle."

"And did this girl finish the puzzle?" Betsy asked.

"Betsy," the minister replied, fixing his gaze with Betsy's face, "*You* are that girl."

"Me?" Betsy cried bewildered, "but I'm just a kid, a kid not allowed in God's puzzle."

"You will be allowed," the minister replied. "In time, others will learn to see you for who you are, come to understand you, and allow you to fit in as part of the puzzle."

"So every time I make a puzzle, am I like God?"

The minister laughed. "I suppose you could say that, but on a far lesser scale."

"Fishies have scales," Betsy said.

The minister laughed again.

"And what about my sister Laura?" Betsy continued. "Is she a puzzle piece too?"

"Yes, your sister is another piece in God's puzzle," Ben replied. "She will find her way. God made you, and sent you here to help her find her place too."

"And I'll be happy?" Betsy asked.

"Yes," the minister smiled, "You will be. Maybe not today, but everybody has moments in their lives when they feel sadness."

"And Laura will be happy?" Betsy asked.

“Yes,” the minister grinned again, “she will be.”

Betsy looked up at Reverend Ben Herb and made a determined, eager smile once again.

“Hey!” Betsy cried. “I feel happy again already. I will make God happy. I will help God finish his puzzle.”

“That's good to hear,” the minister smiled. “Betsy, in addition to you being a piece in God's puzzle, God has also granted you blessings. These blessings are everything, and everyone, you have that make you happy, including your belongings, your family, your friends, even your body. No matter what happens, you will always have your blessings, and nobody can take them away from you, ever.”

“Will I always have you?” Betsy asked. “Will you come again?”

“Yes, I will,” the minister smiled. “I promise to always be here for you, and support you in every way that I can.”

Reverend Ben Herb turned to Betsy's parents. “I think I have helped your daughter as much as I can today.”

“Thank you, Ben,” Megan smiled. “It was lovely having you in our home. I just know today's meeting is going to help Betsy greatly.”

“I might be able to help you in other ways,” Ben explained. “I will arrange for a community or congregation fund for your family, and pray, nightly, that people will feel more compassion for Betsy as the years progress, and that Betsy will find her way in this world.”

The minister turned, once more, to Betsy. “Bye Betsy,” he smiled. “It was lovely seeing you. Thank you for listening to me, and feeling a sense of encouragement.”

“Oh!” Betsy cried. She dashed down the hallway, into her room, and retrieved the chocolate Santa her parents had given to her for Christmas.

"This is for you," Betsy smiled, handing the Santa to the minister.

"For me?" Reverend Ben Herb cried. "Oh Betsy, you shouldn't. That's your Christmas present your parents gave you."

"I want you to have it," Betsy smiled, continuing to hold the Santa in her outstretched hand.

"Well, thank you very much," smiled Ben, taking the Santa. "I'm sure it will taste lovely."

"Carl! Megan!" grinned Ben, facing Betsy's parents. "See you later. Try to make it out to church sometime."

"We will," the parents beamed, as the minister left.

10 A New Future for the Parkers

The years passed, and Laura grew from babyhood to toddlerhood, and then, from toddlerhood to young-childhood. She developed a sound appetite, got toilet-trained, and soon came to an age where she and Betsy could play together.

Betsy was becoming a well-educated, talkative, playful girl, but there was always a brokenness about her; a muted quality, like a piano playing a merry, playful tune with its damper pedal down.

"You want me to teach you how to play Snakes and Ladders, Laura?" Betsy asked one summer's day, when Laura was four and Betsy was seven.

"What's Snakes and Ladders?"

"I'll get the board and teach you," Betsy smiled.

Betsy walked to the corner of the living room where all the games were kept, and picked out the Snakes and Ladders board. She set the board on the coffee table and opened it.

"Every player gets a marker of one color," smiled Betsy. "The players take turns rolling the dice and moving their marker the same number of spaces as the number on the dice."

Betsy demonstrated by rolling the die, which came up four, and moving the yellow marker to the fourth square.

Betsy continued. "If you land on the bottom of a ladder, move your piece to the top of the ladder; if you land on the tail of a snake, move your piece down to the head of the snake. The first player who gets to 100 wins."

"That sounds like fun," Laura smiled. "Let's play."

Betsy chose green and Laura chose red. They took turns rolling the die, moving their pieces, (Betsy moved Laura's piece for her, since the younger girl couldn't count yet) sliding up ladders, slithering down snakes, and eventually Laura's piece arrived at 100, with Betsy's at 72.

"I won!" Laura cried. "Hey Betsy, I'm better than you!"

"Laura! Don't boast!" yelled Megan from the kitchen.

"Sorry," sighed Laura, making a sheepish expression towards Betsy.

Laura and Betsy played together a lot. One time, they played with a princess doll and a witch doll. They pretended that the witch was taking the princess captive, but a Fairy Godmother (a third doll who carried a wand) stepped in and saved the princess in time.

On another occasion (it was a rainy day and the girls were playing inside) they pretended that it rained so much that the rain covered the house, then the trees, and they pretended to swim and swim until they found an island.

When it was sunny and warm outside, Betsy and Laura would sometimes play tag in the back yard. Other times they would splash and play together in Betsy's splash pool, with Laura sometimes unclothed as Betsy was, other times wearing a one-piece yellow bathing suit with little brown polka-dots all over it.

Overall, Laura was sweet like her sister. She loved and accepted Betsy, but she also had a bratty, tantrum-throwing streak. Sometimes, when one of her parents took Laura shopping, she would see something she just had to have, or she kept asking for many different items from the same store. When her mother or father (whichever parent was with her) said 'no' she would often become upset and start crying and screaming.

Other times, she would refuse to eat items of her supper that her parents told her she had to eat, sometimes, so stubbornly that if her parents told her that she wouldn't get any dessert if she didn't eat them, Laura would storm away from the table, hide in her room and act cross for the rest of the evening.

“What's up with Laura?” Megan would sometimes ask. “We never got any of this kind of behavior from Betsy.”

“Oh, she's just a kid being a kid,” Carl answered. “She'll grow out of it eventually.”

Two weeks before Laura was destined to begin kindergarten, she turned to her father. “Daddy, I want you to remove my training wheels ... please.”

Upon hearing this, Carl was delighted, both that his second, more stubborn, daughter had just said 'please' without having to be reminded, and that, at the young age of four-and-a-half years, she was already asking to ride her bicycle on two wheels.

“I'll be happy to remove your training wheels,” her father smiled. “Are you sure you're ready?”

“Yes daddy,” Laura insisted.

Soon, he had told his wife; she was just as delighted as he was, and Carl began removing the training wheels from Laura's bike.

Betsy noticed what was happening to her sister's bike and peered eagerly and excitedly out the living room window.

“Can I come out and see Laura ride?” she asked her mother.

“I'm sorry dear,” Megan sighed. “You'll have to watch from the window.”

Betsy let out, yet another, sigh of disappointment. “Please mom!” Betsy cried. “Just this once? I've never even been out in the front yard in my life.”

“I'm sorry Betsy,” Megan sighed. “The window will have to do. Look, I'll stay by the window and watch with you.”

When the wheels were off, Laura mounted her bike. Carl held onto the handlebars, and Laura tried to pedal it forward. The bike tipped back and forth. Laura pedalled faster, but the bike fell, and down came Laura with it.

“Oh!” cried Megan. “Wait there, Betsy. I'm going to go see if

Laura's all right."

Megan dashed down the stairs, hurried out the door, and a few seconds later, Betsy saw her mother trot down the street, looking Laura over, checking for injuries.

As Betsy watched, the tension built up inside her. Could Laura be badly injured? Was she going to be okay? What if she had a broken bone?

"Don't worry Laura!" Betsy yelled. "I'm coming!"

Betsy dashed away from the window, hurried down the stairs, pulled the door open, and ran onto the side of the street where Laura was lying, upset and somewhat shaken.

"Betsy!" Carl yelled, when he saw his older daughter. "Get back in the house now!"

"But Laura's hurt!" Betsy protested.

"I know it's hard for you Betsy, but you can't come out here like this. Laura's just a little scratched; that's all. She'll be fine."

Disappointed at being talked to this way, Betsy disappeared back into the house.

But Laura didn't give up. Only a few minutes after that first stumble, she tried again, then again the next day, and again the next, and, by the time the last weekend of the summer holidays had arrived, Laura had mastered the skill of riding on two wheels.

"Congratulations Laura!" her mother cried. "How does it feel to be riding on two wheels?"

Laura rushed past on her bike, with her hair in the breeze, wearing an excited smile.

"It feels great mommy! I can't believe I'm doing this!"

She celebrated after with some milk and cookies.

***

On the first day of school, Laura awoke at 8:00, eager and excited for her first day of kindergarten. She grabbed her pink heart backpack, and her mother walked her over to school.

Laura came home from school quiet that day. Her mother picked her up at 3:00, asked her how her day had been, to which the girl replied, “Eh.” Then, when her mother asked Laura what she did, Laura said, “Stuff.” When Megan asked what sort of stuff, Laura cried, “It's okay mom!”

The next day was worse. Laura came home, definitely hurt about something. She didn't say a word after school, or for the rest of the day.

“Hey Laura?” Betsy asked her. “What's wrong?”

Laura's face was angry and red, and she was trembling. “Go away!” she yelled at Betsy.

Saddened and confused, Betsy turned away from Laura and left the room.

On Wednesday, Laura yelled, at the end of the school day, “I won't go back tomorrow!”

When Betsy asked Laura what was wrong, Laura yelled at her sister, “Don't talk to me! Just get away from me!”

When supper came that evening, Laura announced, “I am not sitting at the table if Betsy's there. I won't play with Betsy again. I don't like Betsy anymore!”

Then, without saying another word, and before her parents could stop her, Laura picked her plate up, and headed to the coffee table in the living room.

Megan got up from the table and looked at Laura. Surely enough, Laura was crying.

Megan sat down on the couch and put her arm around Laura. “Laura dear?” Megan asked. “What's wrong?” although deep inside, Megan already knew.

“They're mean,” wept Laura. “The big kids on the playground. They say 'Are you Betsy Parker's little sister?' 'Does your sister have her clothes on?' 'How does your sister look naked?'”

“Those are what we call bullies,” explained her mother. “They tease people because they don't understand what it's like to be someone else. They feel insecure about themselves, so they put others down. If anyone ever says something like that to you, again, tell your teacher. She'll deal with it.”

“Everyone says it,” Laura sobbed.

“Oh Laura, I'm sure it's not everyone. You've seen a lot of people acting this way towards you, but it just seems like everyone because so many are doing it, but I'm sure there are many more kids who would be understanding.”

But Laura was not convinced.

“I was finding a friend, Tommy,” Laura wept. “Today, he stopped being my friend. He looked at me and said 'My friend William's daddy took William out of school because of you.' Tomorrow, I won't come back. Mommy what have I done?”

“You've done nothing, Laura,” Megan explained. “Laura, I feared this would come. I brought you into this world so that Betsy could have company, even if it was just from one other child. I understand it's not very fair to you, Laura, that you are in this situation.”

“So you had me for Betsy?” howled Laura. “You don't want me?!”

“Laura, it's not like that,” Megan insisted. “I love you too.”

But the little girl stormed down the hallway, slammed her door behind her, and burst into tears, howling on her bed.

Betsy heard her sister slam her door and start crying. At that moment, Betsy decided that this was the last straw. She was going to become a real person. She was going to become normal. She was going to put some clothes on.

She stepped away from the dinner table, and headed down the hallway.

"Hey Betsy," Carl asked after his daughter. "Where are you going? Aren't you hungry?"

"I have to do the homework mom gave me," she announced.

Betsy looked in the door of Laura's room for something to wear, but everything was too small. She looked in her parents' room. Everything was too big, but at least a large item could be wrapped around her body.

She opened the wardrobe. There were several dresses inside. There was a red one, a white one, a purple one, a pink one, a mauve one, a turquoise one, and a yellow one.

Betsy gazed at the yellow one. It looked delightful. Betsy knew she would feel delightful if she wore it. All through her childhood, Betsy had wanted to wear clothes. She had dreamed of it. She was finding that the clothing people wore expressed so much about their characters, their moods, their interests, and their bodies. Betsy was determined to become like everyone else, to become accepted, to live like a real human. She was determined to take part in the joy the expression of clothing brought. Wearing nothing but her bare skin all the time was becoming tedious and boring.

She reached up and picked the yellow dress out of the wardrobe. It was an intense, golden yellow, and she knew she would feel like a princess if she wore it. She felt the shoulder. It was silk. Surely, it would be soft and smooth enough on her skin that she wouldn't react.

She deliberately let the hem of the dress brush her belly button. Then, she waited one minute. Nothing happened.

"So far, so good," Betsy mouthed to herself. "I'll be okay. I'm seven years old now. I should be grown out of this curse I've had since I was a baby."

Without wasting another minute, Betsy slipped the dress on.

A jubilant joy of relief erupted inside her. She was free, like a real person, like a princess. She looked in the bedroom mirror and burst out laughing, a happy, girly, bubbly, giggling laugh. It was as though her body was wrapped in gold, instead of the boring, plain skin she'd had to wear all the time, that no other person wanted to see.

"I'm princess Betsy," she cheered, and her reflection smiled back at her, echoing those very same words. "And now I can go out, ride ponies, make friends and go to school. I can ..."

Betsy wheezed.

"Play in the fields all day and ..."

She wheezed again, this time louder and more tightly than before.

"Laura will like me again and ..."

She was losing her breath fast, and now, she was growing dizzy.

"HELP!" she yelled.

She could feel an intense burning sensation on her skin, under the dress.

At this point, she resorted to getting the dress off. She whipped it off so fast that it tore. She saw herself naked, once again, in the mirror, but her whole skin had gone red and bumpy. She also saw that her nose was bleeding. She was so dizzy, she couldn't stand, and she toppled to the floor in a faint.

BANG went the bedroom door as Carl and Megan burst inside, where they had heard Betsy scream for help.

"Hhhhhhhhuh!!!" Megan gasped, when she saw Betsy, lying there, unconscious, the dress, torn, and lying on the bedroom floor at Betsy's side.

“Carl, you stay and watch Betsy, and please give her a dose of her epi-pen!” Megan cried. “I'm calling 911.”

Megan sprinted out of the bedroom and grabbed the phone. “Please dispatch an ambulance!” she called. “My little Betsy is sick again.”

She ran back into the bedroom, and looked her daughter over.

“Oh no no no,” Carl sobbed. His wife was crying too. She had her mouth down to Betsy's and was helping the girl breathe.

At that moment, Laura burst out of her room. “Something happened?” she cried. When Laura saw Betsy, her face turned white, and she stood still, not knowing what to make of this situation.

“Is Betsy okay?” Laura wept.

“She's alive,” said Carl, in a fearful voice, shaking his head, “but she is very very sick. She's not breathing easily, and we don't know if she's going to be okay.”

Laura stepped over to Betsy's side. “Betsy,” Laura sobbed. “I'm sorry.”

Betsy remained still.

“I'm sorry,” Laura wept again, in the most sincere, wistful, apologetic voice she had ever made. “Will that help her?”

“It might,” said Megan. “We can only hope. Thank you for apologizing and thinking of your sister.”

“Maybe the Fairy Godmother will come and make her better,” Laura suggested.

“I'm afraid not dear,” Megan sighed, between giving Betsy breaths. “The Fairy Godmother is only in stories. She's not real.”

“I think she's real,” Laura said.

After what felt like an eternity, the ambulance arrived. The paramedics gave Betsy a breathing mask and prepared her for the trip to the hospital.

“This is the girl we've been hearing about in the news,” one of them commented. "So sorry to see she's had another reaction."

They brought Betsy to the door where the ambulance was parked, and loaded her inside the back of the ambulance. Carl, Megan and Laura bundled in, behind the paramedics, and they drove away, back to the hospital.

When the medics and the Parkers arrived at the hospital, the Parkers brought out Betsy's waterbed and the doctors set her down. There was nothing more for the Parkers to do, but to accompany Betsy in the hospital and hope for the best.

Laura did not go to school the next day. Not only did she not want to be teased, but Laura and her parents agreed that Laura was too traumatized by what had happened to her sister to attend school. All three kept Betsy company. Eventually, Betsy regained consciousness, and said, to her mother,

"Mom, I'm so sorry."

Megan screamed in delight and burst into tears.

"Betsy!" she cried. "You're getting better."

"I shouldn't have worn that dress."

"I know," Megan sobbed. "It's okay Betsy. I forgive you. I'm just so glad you're still here."

"And I'm glad too," Laura grinned.

Betsy was released from the hospital on Sunday. She was still not totally herself. She was disoriented and a little dizzy.

"Mom," Betsy said to Megan when she was back at home. "I promise I will never ever do anything like that again as long as I live."

"I hear you Betsy," Megan breathed in relief. "I know you won't."

"It was stupid, foolish, and selfish. It almost took my life."

"But you are still here," smiled Megan, "You're alive and talking. That's all that matters."

"I only wanted to be a real person," Betsy explained.

"You are a real person Betsy," her mother insisted. "I have told you that so many times."

"But it's not enough," Betsy continued. "I wanted to be accepted, and I still do. I know you accept me; you, dad and Laura ... well Laura most of the time, but it's not enough. You accept me because you're my family. You accept me because you brought me onto Earth. I want to be accepted for real. I am tired of being in this same house all the time, with nothing but the back yard."

Her mother shook her head, "Well Betsy; I can't see what we can do about that."

"And I can't even express myself," Betsy explained. "If I wasn't like this, I'd adore clothing. I know I would. I probably wouldn't even want to go without clothing anymore. Everyone else puts on clothes to show who they are, so they can keep warm in cold places, so they can be people, and I am ... well, I don't know what I am."

"Betsy," her mother reassured her. "You are a person. You do a wonderful job of expressing yourself. There are so many ways in which people can express themselves besides clothing. There's language, facial expressions, writing, music, talents, interests, and best of all, character; character is the way a person expresses himself or herself from the heart. It's how people show their quality and true nature by what they do for other people, how they relate with other people, how they make other people feel. You have an amazing character, Betsy, and that is your greatest gift of expression."

But Betsy's facial expression was still hollow. "But it's not a gift if I can't express it to anyone besides you, dad, and Laura. Is there somewhere I can go where I don't have to wear clothes, where nobody has to wear clothes, where people can be naked all the time if they want to and nobody minds?"

“Oh BETSY!!!” Megan cried.

Megan knew that such places existed, but she had never told Betsy. It was a thought that had passed through Megan's mind, but it had slithered back out like sand in a sieve. Come to think of it, Megan had always had a feeling, deep down, that one day Betsy might ask this very question. 'Nudist colonies' people often called them. Megan didn't even know if such places would admit children, if it would even be legal for them to admit children. Megan had always assumed that 'nudist colonies' only admitted adults, that every person had to be a minimum of eighteen, perhaps twenty-one, years of age to get in.

“Betsy,” Megan sighed. “We don't ask questions like that,” and Megan left the room.

“What is it dear?” Carl asked his wife when he saw her. He knew that something was amiss.

“Betsy's asked about places where people can go without clothes all the time,” Megan sighed, “and I don't know what to tell her.”

Carl didn't look as surprised as Megan had been. “There are resorts where people can do that, you know,” he explained. “I had been starting to wonder if we could take Betsy to one. I know she'd be accepted there.”

“But would she be allowed?” cried Megan. “She's nowhere near eighteen yet, and even if she can go, would it be safe? There are people in this world who prey on children you know.”

“That's what I've been worrying about,” admitted Carl. “But I think if we keep a close eye on Betsy, I don't think any predator is going to pounce; not while we're around.”

But Megan wasn't convinced. “Carl,” she explained. “I wouldn't want any kind of predator to be around our daughter at all, pouncing or not. You seem to have forgotten that not all people are like us. I wouldn't want my wonderful Betsy to be naked around complete strangers, who are also naked, most of whom will be adults."

"Well, it's not like she already hasn't been," Carl explained. "We didn't exactly know the Barnes's when they first came over four years ago."

"Oh, but that's not the same. They're from our neighborhood."

"Megan, nudist colonies, well resorts actually, do admit children. For the past few years, I've done some research about them on the internet, thinking about them as an option for Betsy. I had just never worked up the guts to tell you. The only catch is that the parents have to be there too, to be supervising their children."

"This is wrong," Megan wept. "Carl, this is so so wrong."

"Don't you think it's wrong that Betsy is kept locked up in the house, homeschooled all the time, never allowed any freedom, like she's an animal in the zoo? Our daughter, contrary to what some people have come to think, is not an animal. She's human, and she, just like any other child, is entitled to some happiness."

"But it won't be much of a happy vacation if we're constantly having to watch Betsy," Megan insisted, "and what about Laura? And what about us? I wouldn't want to be naked around so many people I don't know. You and I have never even been completely naked around Betsy."

"You know Megan," Carl sighed. "When Betsy was a little girl, I mean really little, she had an innocence to her, a happiness, a playfulness, a sweetness. Now that she is getting to know the world, and culture's taboos, I can feel that innocence leaking out. Don't you feel it Megan? Betsy used to laugh, run, jump, play. She doesn't do that anymore; she hasn't done that for a couple years now. She is hurt Megan; hurt, bruised, scratched inside. I would do anything to bring that innocence back."

"I know, Carl," Megan wept. "I understand."

"You saw what Betsy did, just last Wednesday, putting that dress on," Carl continued. "That's how desperate she is; she would literally risk her own life to be 'normal.' She did that because she was lonely, confused, sheltered and outcast. Wouldn't you be willing to do anything to keep that from happening again?"

"Of course I would! But Betsy won't do it again. She promised me."

"Megan!" Carl insisted. "Betsy is reaching out to you. She trusts you to help her, to guide her. Don't you want what's best for her?"

"Of course I do, but I'm not sure a nudist colony, er, resort is the answer."

"What is the answer then?" Carl asked Megan.

"Oh!" cried Megan. She sat down, and gave the situation a lot of thought. She thought of Betsy continuing her life, as a homeschooled girl, constantly shut in the house. She thought of Betsy trying on the dress and reacting in the worst way. She thought of Betsy escaping her imprisonment and running outside naked, only to be laughed at, teased, and Carl and Megan being questioned by the police. Then, Megan imagined Betsy outdoors, in a beautiful utopia, surrounded by lush trees, gorgeous grass, playing around naked, happily and freely, with other people just as happy, naked, and innocent as she was, every one of them, truly, completely understanding and accepting of Betsy.

With that thought, Megan gave one more sob, and caved in. "Okay, Carl. You win. We will let Betsy try out a nudist resort, but what about Laura? She doesn't have to be there."

"I think we should take Laura too," Carl explained. "It would help her become more understanding of Betsy, and it would add a happy new dimension to Laura's life."

“But if we take Laura, she'll only get teased at school much more,” Megan protested. “I can, maybe, understand taking Betsy, but only because Betsy is a special case, but any other kid, no way. I don't even think there should be any kids in those places.”

“Laura's teacher and the principal should be dealing with the teasing,” explained Carl, “and if they don't, then it is up to us. Whether we take Laura or not, she is going to face some ridicule. However, if we do take Laura, she will be more likely to stand up for herself and for Betsy, because she will then know, first-hand, what Betsy's situation is like. If we take Betsy, and leave Laura at home with a babysitter, Laura will be far more likely to see Betsy as nothing but an embarrassment, someone who unfairly pulls Laura's own reputation down, an enemy even. Laura won't understand Betsy and will, therefore, lack compassion for her; compassion that Betsy so desperately needs, and was the main reason why we had Laura in the first place. It could culminate in a bitter resentment, even hatred, between our two daughters.”

“I see dear,” contended Megan again, after much thought. “Very well. We will give this a try with both our daughters, but I can't promise you that it's going to work. For all we know, it might even make things worse.”

***

As Carl was coming home from work the next day, he picked up a brochure about travel destinations. He flipped through it and found a naturist resort called 'Sunny Palms.'

11 Betsy's Big Adventure

The Parkers spent a lot of time puzzling over how they were going to get to Sunny Palms. Betsy had never been transported in a car, or anywhere outside the house before.

"What would be the safest way of transporting Betsy to avoid her being seen?" Carl asked his wife.

"This is your idea," she explained. "You should figure it out. What I've been wondering is, what about school? Even on a weekend, we wouldn't be able to be down there long enough to make a worthwhile trip, and the weather is getting cooler."

"Megan, I haven't told you this yet, but Sunny Palms is in Hilo, Hawaii."

Suddenly, Megan spilled her tea down her shirt, and spewed the tea she had in her mouth all across the table.

"HAWAII?!!! ARE YOU INSANE? HOW IN HEAVEN'S NAME DO YOU PLAN TO TRANSPORT BETSY OUT OF VIEW OF THE PUBLIC ALL THE WAY TO HAWAII?! AND WHAT DO YOU PLAN TO DO ABOUT THE GIRLS' SCHOOLING?!"

"We can go during the Christmas break," explained Carl. "The climate isn't even too hot. Sunny Palms is also near the inactive volcano Mauna Kea, so we should see some spectacular sunsets, and spend our time on lush, fertile ground."

"And the transportation?" Megan asked again. "We can't fly, because we would have to go into a public airport and onto a public airplane."

"Hey, I didn't say it was going to be easy," Carl explained, "but there's an old expression that goes 'Where there's a will, there's a way.'"

"And what's the way?" Megan asked.

Carl thought for a minute. "I'll call the resort. Then, I'll call the airport," he said at last.

He, then, dialled Sunny Palms' number, and told them that he was the father of Betsy Parker, the girl whose story had been circulating in the news. The resort staff sounded very friendly. They agreed to let the Parkers come from December 16 to the 21.

Then, he called the airport and told the staff there about Betsy, his plans to take her to Sunny Palms, and ended up engaging in a long discourse about how to transport her. Finally, Carl smiled, and made a leap of joy.

"Thank you!" he smiled. "Thank you so much for thinking of us, and my daughter's needs," and he hung up.

"What happened?" asked Megan, surprised and puzzled. "Surely they haven't agreed to let Betsy come into the airport in her birthday suit."

"No," Carl explained, "but they have agreed to take us from here to Meriton's airport in a private helicopter. Then, the airport will set aside a private plane for us to take us to Hilo's airport. This plane will connect to the helicopter so that we won't have to go into the airport. Then, another helicopter will take us from Hilo's airport to the gate of Sunny Palms. Our airport will send a helicopter to our house on December 16. The airport staff are so happy that Betsy is going to be meeting other people, and so determined to help her succeed that they've also granted a 50% discount to us for this and every subsequent trip, if any, when we take the plane to Sunny Palms."

"That's wonderful Carl!" Megan cried. "I'm very happy that there are some people in the world who are this thoughtful."

Now, all was said and done. All that the Parkers had to do was get ready for their big adventure. Carl and Megan were not particularly worried about the expense, as church and community support groups, which Reverend Ben Herb was helping to organize, were raising a fund in the Parkers' name.

"Hey Betsy!" called Megan to her daughter. "We have agreed to take you to a resort where everyone is naked!"

Betsy came bursting out of the living room to her mother in the kitchen.

"You have?! Oh mommy, thank you! I have never been away from this house in my life, and I will finally get to make some real friends who will understand me!"

"Can I come?" Laura called after her. "I want to go there too."

"Of course you can!" Megan grinned in ecstasy. "We're all going. Mommy, daddy, you and Betsy."

Right after Megan had told her daughters about the resort, Betsy's behavior and mood brightened. Laura, too, was excited. She was playing with Betsy more again and she continued going to school. Laura's teacher did her best to curb the teasing, and to separate Laura from other students she felt might make fun of her.

The Indian summer turned into full-blown autumn; the autumn turned into winter; and before the Parkers knew it, they were flying high in the air, escaping the cold winter and snow that was falling all around. Betsy was sitting on her pad in the plane, while Laura was sitting next to her, looking out the window.

"Whoa," Laura breathed. "We're really high, aren't we?"

"We certainly are," her father explained, "about 12,000 feet."

"I don't know what that means," Laura commented.

Betsy was lost for words.

"This is," she commented at last, "I don't know ... weird."

"Well, it's sure new for you," her father smiled.

"It sure is, and fun, and exciting, and a bit ... scary, being this high above the ground with nothing to support us."

Betsy turned to Laura.

“How are you enjoying yourself Laura?”

Laura was busying herself blowing up a red balloon. She let it grow bigger and bigger. Then, she slammed her hand on it and popped it.

Laura laughed, but everyone else jumped.

“Now you behave yourself young lady,” her mother assured her. “The pilot needs to focus on flying the plane. He needs as little distraction as possible.”

All the Parkers spent much of their time gazing out the window. As they flew along, mountain ranges, forests, grasslands, and rivers drifted past. Betsy, in particular, was so intrigued and fascinated, she could never stop talking.

“There is so much to this world!” she exclaimed. “It's amazing. I love it all. I want to be part of it. There's so much out there I have never seen before. I love all these different sights; the meadows, the mountains, everything.”

“I think you will find that our vacation destination will be the best yet,” her father beamed. “Just you wait. You will love it so much you will never want to go home.”

Eventually, the plane transferred to the second helicopter from Hilo's airport to Sunny Palms, and, later still, the helicopter from Hilo's airport landed. “Here you are!” called the pilot. “I have brought you here safe and sound.”

“Thank you!” the whole family called.

The Parkers found that they had landed on a gravel road, in hot sun, under a clear sky. For a family that had flown in from up North, it was really disorienting that this was actually December. There was already a young woman, still dressed, awaiting their arrival at the gate. She was smiling at the Parkers.

“Welcome, all of you,” she beamed at the foursome at the gate. “I am Susan Carson. Come on in. I'll get the gate open for you.”

She undid a latch, and, walking the gate behind her, pulled it open.

"Well, looks like you're all ready to get settled," nodded the pilot. "I will see you all in five days."

He started the motor of his helicopter, pulled some switches and flew off.

"Come on in and get settled," smiled Susan at everyone.

"What about us?" Megan asked. "My husband and I are new to this, and we are not sure we would feel comfortable about getting undressed."

"Not to worry," Susan assured her. "We have had many newcomers come here, and they find that they very quickly feel comfortable being undressed. You will have some time to remain clothed, as this is your first time, but you will be expected to be undressed after a few hours."

"I appreciate your thoughtfulness," Megan continued, "but if it hadn't been for our daughter, Betsy, my husband and I would never have dreamed of coming to a place like this, and if anyone had even suggested the idea, I know we would have turned it down. Can you make an exception for us to let my husband and I remain clothed all the time?"

Despite Megan's reservations, Susan remained happy and welcoming. "You will quickly find that if you stay clothed, you will feel out of place and self-conscious. I can almost guarantee there will come a time when you won't even want to keep your clothes on anymore. Please come inside. I will show you around."

Susan stepped forward into what the Parkers perceived as a tropical garden of paradise. There were palm trees, papaya trees, mango trees, banana trees, with a rich, lush lawn underfoot. The sky was a stunning blue, and the sun's warmth hugged them all.

There was a pool, where several nudists, including two families with children, were swimming. Beside the pool was a ping pong table.

"This is our pool," Susan explained. "It is clothes-free. No bathing suits, or any other attire, are allowed in the pool."

Susan turned to a small tub next to the pool.

"This is the hot tub."

And then, she turned to another small pool next to the hot tub.

"This," Susan explained, "is for your daughter Betsy. When you told us about Betsy, we felt it would be necessary to install a pool specifically for her needs. It is non-chlorinated, so it should be suitable for her skin."

Carl and Megan's eyes grew wide in amazement.

"Oh, thank you!" cried Betsy. "Thank you so much for thinking of me. I was wanting to go swimming, but I thought I wouldn't be able to with chlorine in the water."

"You are very welcome," smiled Susan to Betsy. "You seem like such a wonderful little girl. I know you are going to live a good life."

Susan led the Parkers to a tennis court.

"This is where we play tennis," Susan explained. "We have many rackets, tennis balls, and birdies set up at the side."

Then, Susan showed the Parkers a small cabin. It was a pretty, comfortable place. Its walls were made of logs, and there was a cedar smell in the air. It had a quaint kitchen, complete with fridge, stove, table, and a window, with curtains, to view the outdoors. Adjacent to the kitchen were two sets of washrooms, with a bath, shower, and fully functioning toilets.

"Mr. and Mrs. Parker," Susan smiled. "Just down the hall, here, is a bedroom for both of you."

Across from the parents' room, was a smaller room with an individual bed.

“You can sleep here, Laura,” explained Susan.

Over the course of the next fifteen minutes, the Parkers unloaded their supplies. They filled the fridge with their food, set up their toiletries, and filled Betsy's waterbed. Then, they brought the waterbed into the room across from Laura's.

“Hey, I'm going out!” Betsy called, when the unpacking was done.

“Me too!” shouted Laura, and Laura pulled off her shoes, socks, pants, underwear, and shirt, and went running out naked, screaming in delight!

“Hey! Wait for me!” Betsy called after her sister.

“Come back here!” shouted their mother. “You're not going out without our supervision.”

But, already, both girls were running and dancing in their bare skin.

“I love this!” Betsy cried, running around in circles. “I've been wishing I could live, just like this, all my life.”

“But you do,” Laura corrected her.

Betsy paid no attention, but took off towards the pool.

“I'm going to meet some of the other kids at last!” she shouted after Laura.

“Hey! Wait up!” shouted Carl and Megan together, as they stepped out the cabin door. “We will all go down to the pool together, after we put some sunscreen on Laura.”

Betsy heard the bit about the sunscreen and stopped dead in her tracks.

“Should I wear sunscreen too?” inquired Betsy. “Won't the sun burn my skin?”

“I talked to the doctor,” explained Carl. “He cannot guarantee that sunscreen will be safe on you. I'm sorry Betsy, but you're going to have to limit your time out in the sun, to keep from getting sunburned. You can play in the pool for half an hour, but then, we will ask you to come back into the cabin."

Nonetheless, Betsy remained cheerful and eager. "I want to see the pool!" she cried in joy. "Let's go for a swim!"

The Parkers put sunscreen on Laura, made their way to the pool, Mr. and Mrs. Parker still dressed, with Betsy and Laura in the lead.

Betsy dipped her feet in the non-chlorinated pool much as she had done in her splash-pool when she was a toddler.

"I love this," Betsy beamed. "I'm so happy that the people here are thinking of me."

"It's great to see you are enjoying it," her mother smiled. "I am so glad."

Laura stepped into the water and had a little wade. She didn't say anything, but she smiled, and it was obvious that she was enjoying herself.

Another blonde-haired girl, about Betsy's age, noticed Betsy from the main pool and got out. She walked to Betsy's pool and stepped in.

"Hey, I've heard of you," smiled the other girl, with interest and sincerity. "You're Betsy Parker."

"I am Betsy," she beamed. "This is such a wonderful place."

"My name is Catherine," the other girl smiled.

At that moment, Laura spoke up.

"I'm Laura! I'm Betsy's sister, and I'll be five in February!"

"Well, good for you," Catherine grinned. "I'm eight; eight-and-a-half."

At that moment, a dragonfly fell into the water.

"Don't worry," Betsy smiled lovingly. "I'll save you."

She reached forward and pulled the dragonfly out of the water. It flew off, unharmed.

"Wow!" cried Catherine. "That was so kind of you. You really have a heart for living things."

"I do," Betsy continued, smiling all the while. "My mom says that, when I was just two, I rescued a fly from a cup of lemonade I was drinking."

"That's wonderful," grinned Catherine. "Betsy, there are some lovely trails in the woods. Would you like to go for a walk there? I've had enough pool."

"That would be great," cried Betsy. "We can go now. I've always wanted to see what it's like in the woods."

Betsy turned to her parents.

"Mom! Dad! Are you coming?"

"Betsy, Laura is just getting used to the pool."

"I'll go," called Laura. "I want to see the woods too."

Laura hurried out of the pool, and faced the grass and trees at the edge of the lawn, like she was eager and ready to go.

Betsy and Catherine, too, were eager to go for a walk in the woods together. They climbed out of the pool and Catherine's mother turned to Betsy and her parents.

"My name is Nancy," she smiled. "I'm Catherine's mom. We live here in Hawaii. We read about this place in a magazine, inquired about it, and here we are. We have found that we love it."

"I am so glad," Carl smiled. "I'm Carl, and this is my wife, Megan. I read about Sunny Palms in a travel brochure when I was looking for somewhere we could take Betsy to meet other people."

With their plans all set, Carl, Megan, Betsy, Laura, Nancy and Catherine stepped outside the pool facility and out into the open lawn.

"You know," breathed Megan, "I'm getting hot." Megan removed her shoes, socks and shirt and put them on a nearby rock. Then, she looked down, and with an expression of hesitation and uncertainty in her face, removed her pants and underwear as well.

"Wow!" cried Carl. "You're bold. You were the one who was the most hesitant to come here."

"I feel bold," Megan announced. "That's why I'm fitting in. I felt really out of place on the pool deck back there."

In another minute, Carl was undressed too.

"This feels really strange," he commented. "Do you think this is how it feels to be Betsy?"

"No," Megan replied. "She's been this way all her life and it's all she ever knows."

"Well, looks like we're all set," Nancy smiled. "Into the woods it is then."

They stepped across the grass. It felt smooth and cool under their bare feet.

"This feels ... weird," stuttered Megan. "There's a voice inside my head that's telling me 'you need to put some clothes on' but I'm actually finding this quite cool, natural and almost comfortable even. Not sure if I could live my life here, or do this sort of thing every day though."

When they reached the borderline of the woods, Betsy ran and jumped in joy. "I have never felt anything like this!" she cried. "This feels amazing!"

The families found themselves sheltered under a canopy of trees, with a multitude of dividing branches and green leaves overhead. There was a warm breeze in the air that was hugging and caressing them all.

Here, the grass ended to bring a path of dusty soil under everyone's feet. They took a slow stroll through the first path they could find. The light wind was making the trees sway, giving them a creaking sound, as they sidled back and forth. The wind was rustling the leaves, in a way that sounded as sweet as welcoming chimes.

Stepping through this forest made them feel like creatures of the woods, a part of nature, happy, serene and pure. A butterfly flitted past and lighted upon a palm leaf.

For a long time (nobody could know exactly how long, for time seemed to have gone on pause) these six people stepped quietly, and peacefully through the paths in the forest, gazing up into the trees, gazing down the path ahead of them, looking at the bushes around them, and rocks covered in moss. They all remained silent, never saying a word, no one wanting to disturb the peace and freedom of this enchanting forest.

At some point, they turned around and headed back in the direction they had come, subconsciously, as though the turn-around was a natural part of the walk. When they found themselves back at the green pavilion of the campsite, they were nothing less than thrilled.

"I loved that walk!" Carl cried. "Thank you for wanting to go for a walk in the woods, Betsy."

"You're welcome dad," Betsy smiled back at him.

"Did you enjoy that, Betsy?" Catherine asked.

"I loved it," Betsy breathed, in peace. "Deep down, this is what I have always wanted, my whole life."

"How's your skin feeling, Betsy?" her mother asked her.

"It's good," Betsy answered. She looked at her arms and legs to find that they were slightly tanner than normal.

"Do you want to go inside, to get some shade? You don't want to get sunburned."

"I can stay out a bit longer," Betsy replied. Then, she turned to Catherine.

"Hey Catherine!" Betsy beamed. "You want to play frisbee?"

"I love frisbee," Catherine smiled. "Sure, I'll play with you, Betsy."

“Okay!” called Betsy. “Back in a bit.”

Betsy and her mother returned to the cabin where the Parkers were staying. Betsy pulled her frisbee out of the family's luggage bag, and ran back onto the lawn to play with Catherine.

With a smile and a giggle on Betsy's face, she threw the frisbee to Catherine. Catherine jumped and caught the frisbee as it sailed to her. Catherine threw the frisbee to her mom, who threw it to Megan, who threw it to Carl, who threw it to Laura, who threw it back to Betsy.

And so, a pleasurable game of frisbee ensued, with each person running or jumping to catch the spinning disk, before throwing it to another person.

Even Laura was having a blast. Despite her young age, and short stature, she caught on fast, and was becoming a great catcher and thrower, just like everyone else.

Soon, it was suppertime. The Parkers headed into their cabin, while Catherine and her mother made their way towards their trailer.

The Parkers prepared a sumptuous meal of spaghetti and meatballs, which was Betsy's all time favorite meal.

“You like it here?” Betsy's mother asked.

“Like it? I love it. I wish I could live here always.”

Her parents knew this wouldn't be practical, but they smiled and laughed all the same. They gazed at Betsy. When they looked at their daughter, they could see that she was happy and at ease once again.

***

The next day brought more fun adventures: another swim in the little pool with Catherine and another walk in the woods. Then, that afternoon, Susan called all the children in the resort to the patio to make arts and crafts.

Betsy made a drawing of a sunny sky over a deep blue lake; Laura made some finger-puppets; Catherine made a sock puppet of a dragon.

“Betsy!” cried Catherine, as she looked at Betsy's drawing. “That is amazing. You can draw very well for your age.”

“Thanks Catherine,” smiled Betsy.

The next day was sundae making and a treasure hunt. In all this time, with Betsy staying in the hot, tropical sun, she was noticing something interesting. Although she never put on a dab of sunscreen, her skin was not burning at all. In fact, it had darkened into a rich tan.

Her parents noticed this also. “Wow Betsy!” Carl grinned at one point. “That's a beautiful tan you're getting there.”

“It sure is,” Betsy beamed. “And I'm proud of it!”

Her parents laughed, as Betsy dug into her vanilla sundae, which she had decorated with chocolate sauce, chocolate chips and sprinkles.

Betsy spent a lot of time with Catherine over the course of her stay. They played tag on the lawn, played in the sprinkler, played hide and seek, and, on the last day of Betsy's stay, just for fun, came over to Catherine's trailer and made another sundae.

On the last day, before it was time for Betsy to go home, the party of six took one more walk in the woods all together.

Now, at 3:00 in the afternoon of December 21, Carl turned to Betsy. “We have to go home now. Would you like to say one last goodbye to Catherine?”

Betsy stepped towards her friend. “I have to go home now, Catherine,” she explained in a joyful voice, mingled with a trace of disappointment at having to leave so soon. “I promise to return when I can.

"Here," Betsy smiled. She wrote down her phone number on a piece of paper, and handed it to Catherine. "Please call me sometime."

"I will," beamed Catherine. "You're a great friend, Betsy, and a wonderful child. I look forward to seeing you again."

And so, on that day, Betsy Parker and her family returned to the winter land of her home. Betsy, with renewed confidence, asked the Barnes's children to her house every weekend, who were always eager to come and play with her. In fact, Betsy adored the heavenly paradise of Sunny Palms so much that the Parkers returned on Spring Break, then at the beginning of Summer Holidays, then at the end of Summer Holidays, then again during Christmas Holidays. And those journeys, coupled with Betsy's education, was how Betsy thrived year after year after year.

12 Betsy's Grown-up Home

Laura was losing interest in Sunny Palms. She had come with the Parkers routinely since their first visit when Betsy was seven. However, when Laura got to be eleven years old, she asked to be left at home, under the care of the Nelsons. Apart from her family, nobody in Laura's milieu took part in nudism, and Laura could not sway any of her friends to give it a try either. Sometimes, she got teased as well.

"Hey, do your parents have enough money to buy you any clothing?" some children would taunt.

"You don't still go to that place with your naked sister Betsy, do you?" others chided.

Laura tried to cope with the teasing. She would inform these children that the people at Sunny Palms were caring and happy, and that it was just a camp site. Despite this, many still laughed at her, and otherwise mocked her. Additionally, more parents were withdrawing their children from Laura's school, for the sole reason that Laura was the sister of the girl who couldn't be clothed.

And so it happened that Laura no longer wanted to come to Sunny Palms. For the last couple of visits in which Laura came, she seemed quiet, shy, distanced and withdrawn from the other people. Finally, when she was eleven, and it was early June, the beginning of summer vacation, Laura announced, "I won't come to Sunny Palms. None of my friends want to come, kids tease me and I look weird."

"Very well," Megan replied. "We won't force you to come then, if you don't want to."

So the Parkers left Laura at home, where the Nelsons supervised her.

Four years later, when Laura was fifteen, and Betsy was

eighteen-and-a-half, Laura turned, once again, towards resenting Betsy. It was a bright, sunny day in July, in their home town, when Laura turned to Betsy and said, “Hey Betsy, can't you move out?”

“What?” Betsy cried.

“I don't want you here anymore,” Laura groaned. “You're naked all the time, and it's embarrassing.”

“But I'm your sister,” protested Betsy. “I have never done anything to hurt you, nor anyone.”

“What does that have to do with anything?” sighed Laura. “Look Betsy, I keep my body to myself; it's private, and that's the way I want it to be. I will only ever share my body with one other person, and that's the man whom I will love, when I meet him, the man I intend to marry. I don't want to be naked around anybody else, I don't want to see anybody else naked either, and that includes you.”

Betsy let out a sigh of hurt and disappointment. She knew this day was going to come; she could feel it brewing for years. At the same time, Betsy couldn't fathom how she was going to move out. She didn't have a job, nor had she ever had one. Any job that she would be able to undertake would require coming out into the public, into the human world, which was, for Betsy, out of the question. As for education, she was no longer being homeschooled, but, instead, had been watching and listening to her classes over a video link, positioning herself so that only her face was visible from her teachers' end, since her parents had finished teaching her seventh grade. Carl and Megan did not possess the qualifications to teach eighth grade and beyond, so they started Betsy in a program where the local high school had donated a computer to Betsy, so that she could watch and listen to her teachers on video and submit her homework in an envelope that her parents brought to the school.

As soon as Betsy began the regular school curriculum, she was a straight-A student, in every subject, in every term, with marks even higher than Laura's. Whenever Laura needed it, Betsy helped Laura with her homework. Occasionally, a high school student, or two, would be sympathetic enough to come to Betsy's house to visit her. Despite all this, Betsy's schooling was the ultimate ostracizing. Not being able to make friends in the normal way spoiled the satisfaction Betsy would have felt from her academic accomplishments, and she wished that she could, at least once, meet a teacher face-to-face.

This past year, she had graduated from high school, but she'd had to miss the carpet walk, and the dinner and dance. Her high school diploma was delivered to her in the mail. Over the years, Betsy had taken to listening to the mermaid Ariel's song "Part of Your World." Betsy sympathized Ariel with every listening to that song, and she felt nothing more than a human Ariel, longing for just one day in the real human world.

"You love Sunny Palms," Laura continued. "Perhaps you could move there."

"But don't you love me?" Betsy asked.

"Of course I do, but; oh Betsy, I just want my space. That's all. I want to be able to go about my life without a naked butt in my face."

"If I move in to Sunny Palms, will you ever come and visit me?" Betsy asked.

Laura thought for a minute. "I don't know, Betsy. I'll see."

***

That evening, Betsy told her parents of the discourse between her and Laura, and how Laura wanted Betsy to move to Sunny Palms permanently.

"This is a very difficult situation, Betsy," her mother replied. "Why don't we have a family meeting after supper, and we'll discuss what can be done about it."

After the Parkers had eaten supper, Megan cleared the table and Carl washed the dishes. Once the table had been cleared and cleaned, Carl and Megan sat on either end of the table, with Laura sitting at the side and Betsy sitting on her pad next to Laura.

Megan turned to Laura first. "Please tell us what's the matter."

Laura sighed. "I want my privacy; I want my space. Mom, you keep saying that everyone is different, and that includes Betsy, but there's acceptable different, and there's unacceptable different. Betsy is unacceptable different."

"I understand how hard it is for you, Laura," Megan acknowledged, "But you must understand the situation from Betsy's point of view. I'm sure it's equally hard for her, if not more so."

"I'm happy when I'm at Sunny Palms," Betsy explained, "but I'm also happy with you, dad and Laura. If I moved to Sunny Palms, I would miss you all, and I'm only eighteen."

"I know," Carl replied. "Many eighteen-year-olds, if not most, still live at home with their parents, but this is such a difficult situation, Betsy. Laura wants to not be around you anymore, but you want to be here with your family. To be honest, Betsy, if you moved out now, your mother and I would miss you terribly."

"And I would miss you," Betsy responded, "and I would miss Laura."

Betsy turned to face Laura.

"Laura, I don't want to leave you. You're the only full-time playmate and friend I have ever had."

"I've enjoyed playing with you, Betsy," Laura assured her, "but I'm not a little kid anymore. I have a reputation, and it's at stake, and it's not fair. Parents have taken their kids out of my school because I'm your sister, and it's not my fault."

"Do you think it's anymore my fault that I have eosinophilic externitis?" Betsy asked. "My reputation is also at stake because of something I can't help. Don't you and I walk in the same shoes, Laura?"

"No, we don't!" Laura cried. "I wear clothing, but I'm still treated like a freak and a laughing stock. Sometimes, I wish I were an only child, or that I could have a normal sister."

Laura turned to her parents. "Can I be excused? I want to be on my own for a while."

Without waiting for an answer, Laura left the table and shut herself in her room.

For the next few minutes, silence fell upon the table, in which the three remaining parties contemplated their next move. It was Betsy who broke the silence.

"I'll go," she said.

"Go?" asked her mother. "Go where?"

"To Sunny Palms. If it's really going to make Laura's life better, I will move there."

"So you'll live there?" asked Betsy's father. "How will you make a living? How will you pay for your accommodations?"

"Catherine works as a pet groomer. She's always been a good friend. I'm sure she wouldn't mind helping to support me."

"That won't be enough," Carl told Betsy. "You and Catherine are both so young. You don't have a steady income yet."

"I know," said Betsy, "but with the way I am, I don't see how I can get a job."

Another period of silence passed before Megan spoke to Betsy. "We'll help you, Betsy. We can send you money to help pay for your living arrangements. But I must ask you one question: is this really what you want?"

Betsy's mind fell into a swarm of thoughts. She thought of continuing to live with her parents and Laura, in which Laura continued to act upset and embarrassed towards Betsy, as long as Betsy remained under her family's roof. Her parents wouldn't mind. They loved Betsy purely, openly and wholeheartedly. At the same time, Betsy now knew that Laura would mind, that Betsy's presence would continue to eat away at the sisterly bond that had once drawn Betsy and Laura together. It was tragic, but perhaps the only way to rekindle that bond would be to give Laura what she wanted: some time to spend, away from Betsy, to think, grow and learn to feel compassion for the way Betsy lived. Betsy thought of living in the lush greenery at Sunny Palms, with Catherine, Susan and the many other people with whom she enjoyed spending her time. She would miss her parents, and Laura, for sure, but Carl and Megan would always be there for her. Maybe, one day, Laura might do the same.

"It is what I want," Betsy replied, in a final, decided voice.

Carl nodded his head. "That settles it then. When do you want to make the move to Sunny Palms?"

"I'll email Susan," Betsy explained. "We will set up a date that gives me time to pack and we'll arrange for the helicopters and plane to take me over. I'll send you postcards; I promise."

"Well, my dear girl," Megan smiled at Betsy, "That is a really big decision for you to come to. I can tell that you have thought about this a lot. I am so proud of you. Your father and I will come to visit you as often as we can. We will also accompany you when you fly over, and help you get settled when you arrive at Sunny Palms."

"Thank you," Betsy smiled. "That would help me feel so much better. Can I please be excused from the table? I want to go see Laura. I'll tell her my plans and try to comfort her."

"Are you sure?" Carl asked. "Laura left the table because she was uncomfortable with you. You're only going to make her worse."

"I just want to let her know that I have decided to move to Sunny Palms," Betsy explained. "Besides, I'm good at finding the right words if I have some time to think about it. I know I can't make her feel comfortable with me again right at this moment, but I think I can reassure her, just a little."

"All right Betsy," her father smiled. "You're excused."

Betsy left the table and stepped out of the kitchen, walked down the hallway, and knocked on Laura's bedroom door.

"Come in," came a soft, timid voice from inside.

Betsy opened the door and, still standing in the doorway, turned to face Laura who was sitting on the edge of her bed, looking at the floor. Laura wasn't crying, but it was clear that she was depressed and lost.

"Laura," Betsy began, "I'm really sorry your life has come to this. You're right. It's not your fault I'm so different."

Laura looked up from the floor and faced Betsy, her face still downcast, but already showing the first hint of reassurance.

"I know," replied Laura. "Look, Betsy. I'm sorry I got so upset with you. I'm even sorry I walked away from the table like that. It's just that my world is falling apart, and it's all because of you. Oh Betsy, every time I see you ... like that ... I can feel my privacy being invaded, like you're a spectacle being shoved in my face. I know it's not your fault, and I know I shouldn't be mad at you, but I can't help but to be mad at you ... and embarrassed as well."

"I understand," Betsy replied. "Laura, it's okay to be embarrassed, maybe a little mad even. It's natural. Much of the time, that's exactly how I feel. I'm often mad that I'm afflicted with this condition and embarrassed that it's keeping me from living a normal human life. You and I are more alike than you realize, Laura. I believe that, one day, you will come to discover that."

For once, Laura smiled. "I love you, Betsy. I wouldn't want anything to happen to you."

After hearing that statement from Laura, Betsy stepped into

Laura's room and stood in front of where Laura was sitting on her bed.

"I love you too Laura," Betsy smiled back. "Laura, I have decided to move to Sunny Palms. I have given the matter a lot of thought, and you're right. You need your space, and I could use mine too. Now that I think of it, I want to see more of the world, do more, and lead a more independent life."

"I think it will be good for you," Laura replied. "Betsy," she sighed, "I wish I could say that I'll come and visit you, but I wouldn't feel comfortable entering those grounds again, the grounds that have caused me so much bullying and mockery. I want to see you again, but I don't want to look weird."

"You are not weird, Laura, and don't let anyone make you think that. We are all born naked and unashamed. I was, you were; even the people who oppose me, who make fun of you, were."

"I know," said Laura, "but I'm fifteen years old now. Some things are meant to be outgrown. Nudity has a different meaning for me now, from when I was a little girl."

"I've never forgotten the days when you were a little girl, and we used to play together," explained Betsy. "Ever since my childhood, I have found myself wishing that the Fairy Godmother would come down and take my allergy away."

"That's very sad to hear," Laura acknowledged, "but unfortunately, the Fairy Godmother isn't real. Hey Betsy, I've noticed how you have been brushing a towel on your arm, once every couple of years or so, since you wore your mother's dress, to test if you're still allergic. Your parents and I haven't made a fuss about it, since it is an understandable behavior. It hasn't done you any severe harm. Maybe you could try putting something on."

Betsy shook her head. "A rash comes up every time I brush my arm with a towel, and it's itchy, sometimes painful. Even if my allergy wasn't fatal anymore, there would be no way I could stand living with something like that all over my body forever. Besides, I recently stopped that exercise after that latest reaction last winter that sent me back to the hospital for one afternoon. If I were to wear clothes, even now, there's no doubt I would get sent back to the hospital. I might even die."

"I don't want you to die," said Laura. "Betsy, I will come with you and your parents when you move in at Sunny Palms. I might come and visit you, but the discomfort is really getting to me, and I don't think I'm as brave as you are."

"You're my sister, Laura," smiled Betsy, "and that is all that matters, and I honestly think you're quite brave."

"You really think that?" asked Laura, in an intrigued, somewhat surprised voice. "Nobody has ever called me brave before."

"I really do," Betsy smiled. "You came with us to Sunny Palms all those years even when you knew your peers at school wouldn't understand; you tried to stand up for yourself, your family, your fellow campers, and me by trying to convince those schoolmates that Sunny Palms is a friendly, worthwhile place to be; and now, even though you're embarrassed by me, you're still determined to accept me as much as you can and stay my sister."

"I'm glad you feel that way," replied Laura.

"Laura," Betsy explained. "I better let Susan know that I'm moving to Sunny Palms. I'll rent a cabin, and, at least for the first little while, mom and dad and possibly Catherine will help pay for me."

"Good luck," Laura beamed.

Betsy made one more smile at Laura, turned away from Laura's bedside and stepped out of Laura's room. Betsy entered her own room, turned on her computer, and composed an email to Susan detailing her plans of moving to Sunny Palms.

After Betsy had told Susan she was moving out, her parents arranged the plane ride. Two weeks later, when the helicopter arrived to take the Parkers to Meriton's airport, Betsy packed her books, her toiletries and all her belongings. Then, all four Parkers stepped into the cockpit and the helicopter departed.

13 A Bold Decision

When the Parkers arrived at Sunny Palms, Betsy's parents and Laura helped her unpack. They unloaded her bag and her toiletries into her newly rented cabin. They unpacked the cooler and loaded the food into the fridge.

Susan was pleased, as usual, to see Betsy, and excited that Betsy was now here, at Sunny Palms, to stay.

“So, you're living here now, Betsy,” Susan smiled. “It's so wonderful at this place. You'll love making it your permanent home, and we've been so happy to have you here every time you've come.”

Betsy didn't know what to say. “That's very kind of you,” she replied, “but to be honest, I'm nervous and I know I'm going to be lonely.”

“That's normal for people who move out,” Susan reassured her, “but things will work out, I promise.”

Once Betsy was settled, her parents waved to her and called out their farewells.

“See you soon!” they waved. “Happy moving out, and be sure to live a grand life.”

“Mom!” Betsy called, “Dad! You'll come and visit me often, won't you?”

“Of course we will,” Carl smiled. “We look forward to seeing you when that time comes.”

“Bye Laura!” Betsy called.

Laura was waving her hand more faintly and slowly, “Bye Betsy,” she said, in a smaller, more shy voice.

As the three bundled into the helicopter, Betsy gazed at her parents and her sister, especially her sister, for as long as she could. Then, the helicopter rose up, high above the trees, hills and planes, until it was high up in the heavens, and Betsy's family was out of sight.

After her parents and Laura had left, Betsy did not feel the carefree pleasure she usually felt when she came with her family. Betsy was aching to see Catherine. Even after all these years, the bond between Betsy and Catherine had not worn away, but had, instead, grown stronger.

Betsy caught sight of Catherine, sitting on the poolside, and Betsy was so eager to see her, that she ran up to her friend right away.

"Oh Catherine!" Betsy cried. "I'm so happy to see you!"

By now, Betsy was crying, something she had never done at Sunny Palms before, not out of negative feelings, anyway.

"Betsy, what's wrong?!" cried Catherine.

Betsy didn't touch the water, or sit down on her silicon pad beside Catherine, but she stood there, talking to her friend. "I've moved out," Betsy sighed. "I'm on my own now. I don't know what my future is going to be, or what I'm going to do. I don't even know if I will even see my family again."

"Betsy," Catherine answered. "Everybody moves out at some point. Of course you'll see them again. What ever makes you think you won't?"

"I don't know. Because they're ashamed of me?"

"What? Betsy, that's nonsense! Who could ever be ashamed of you?"

"My sister Laura. You've met her before, but she hasn't come here for several years. She says I'm an embarrassment."

Catherine sighed. "Betsy," she soothed. "Just because someone says you are something, doesn't necessarily mean that is what you are. You are a bright, smart young woman with a loving heart."

But, for once, not even Catherine's comfort could satisfy Betsy. “I want to be part of the real world,” Betsy explained. “I want to take part in human society. I want people to accept me for who I am. When I first came here, many years ago, I thought I had got that wish fulfilled, but now I know that was just my imagination. Of course you lot accept me because you're nudists. Of course my family accepts me because they're my family. I want to be accepted for real. I've got to have a taste of the real human world, even if it's just for one day. One day would be better than never at all.”

Catherine looked like she didn't know what to say. “Betsy,” asked Catherine. “Have you ever mentioned this issue, of wanting to be accepted by society as a whole, to your parents?”

“I have,” she explained. “You see, I always got A's in school; I even helped Laura with her homework. Laura goes to school because she's normal, but all Laura wants now is a normal sister; a sister she can never have.”

Betsy turned away from Catherine and gazed off into the distance. “And I had to miss my grad walk, and grad dinner and dance because of the way that I am, and what point is my A education going to be if I can never get a job, or do anything useful for society?”

Catherine continued to try to comfort Betsy. “Did your parents ever have any suggestions? Any at all?”

Betsy thought for a few minutes. Then, she said, “Well, my father recently told me that he said, when I was a baby and my condition was first discovered 'We will fight the law tooth and nail. Nobody is shutting our Betsy away.'”

“And did he ever do that?”

“Yeah, you could say that. My parents have told me all about those legal struggles. My mother has always had reservations; she thinks that getting me the privilege to go out in public will attract creeps who would look at me inappropriately. On the other hand, my father has always believed that other people, at least in my neighborhood, would feel too sympathetic towards me, and too happy for me, that I'm allowed a bit of freedom, to look at me in an inappropriate manner. My parents came to a compromise that they would lobby for me to have the right to be able to explore everywhere inside my own neighborhood, but that was it. My parents let the press know about my situation when I was three years old. Shortly after my story ran in the paper, my father sent a letter to the preliminary court in my local home town. The first letter never got a response. My father sent a second letter, and the local Magistrate Hugh Humphrey acknowledged that, as concerning as my situation was, it was not worth making a case about; that one person's rights, even due to an uncontrollable medical situation, could not overturn the rights and the norms of an entire society."

"And was that the end?"

"Not exactly. After those efforts, my father got in touch with our local police department to ask if it really would be a grievous breach of law for me to have any time, anywhere in public, to be the way I am. The police informed my father that my condition was interesting in that it created a conflict within the Equal Protection Clause of the Bill of Rights. On one hand, everyone is equal under the law, making it unconstitutional for me to have the right to live unclothed, while anyone else would get arrested for doing so. On the other hand, the clause also guarantees no denying of life or liberty, making it unconstitutional for me to be sheltered and hidden from society because of my allergy, while everyone else is allowed to live, openly and freely, the way they are.

"My parents then tried for a compromise in which they hired a lawyer, and mailed a request to the next highest court, for me to have a day to have a walk, just within my neighborhood, but the court, again, declined to hear the case."

Catherine paused for a few minutes before she spoke up. "You know, Betsy, this may sound really odd, and I cannot promise it will work, but maybe, just maybe, *you* could do just that. Fight the law. Get your freedom. Get your rights as a human being."

Betsy shook her head. "They'll never allow it. Catherine, that's the whole problem. I live in a society where every person is required, under penalty of law, to wear clothing in public. Unless that entire societal attitude changes, I will never be able to have that right."

"Maybe not all the time," Catherine explained, "but, hey, you said it yourself. 'Even if it's just for one day.' You could take your case to court and arrange for one day to get a taste of human society, one day in which you will be immune to indecent exposure charges."

"One day," breathed Betsy thoughtfully. "Yes, I think I could try that. It's not as though I'm trying to sway the law to let me go without clothes all the time. If I win, surely there will be a news announcement about it, so that people will be able to stay home if they don't feel comfortable, and even if I lose, I will be able to say I at least tried."

Following Betsy's discussion with Catherine, Betsy picked out one of the postcards her father had purchased for her, and she wrote the following message.

Dear Mom, Dad and Laura,

I have settled in at Sunny Palms. It's so quiet here right now; it's a gorgeous day, and Catherine was happy to see me. I have had a discussion with her in which I have agreed to take the issue of my allergy to court, to win one day in which I can explore human society. I want to see and learn about the real human world, and hopefully meet some people, more the average sorts of citizen. Mom, dad, thank you for trying to get a right like that granted for me when I was a little girl. I understand it didn't work, but at least you tried, and I am proud of you for that. If that same voice comes from me, in person, maybe then, I will win that right. All the same, if I don't, I will accept that. One day, I might find some self-employed work. I don't know what, maybe selling something, and I could find someone like Susan or Catherine to sell it for me. Please come by and visit me sometime. I miss you all.

Sincerely, Betsy

She sealed the envelope and dropped it in at the office.

14 Betsy Speaks her Voice

For Betsy, taking her case to court was easier said than done. She had come to live at Sunny Palms with her parents' money, with Catherine helping to pay for her expenses. Betsy couldn't fathom how she could afford a lawyer. She felt like she was cornered in her life; in a place where she wasn't welcome at home, was only welcome at Sunny Palms with others paying for her, all the while having the urge to come out in public which (whether or not it worked at all) would involve an expensive court case. Betsy couldn't even ask for Catherine's assistance on this issue. She had to talk to someone with more background, more experience. She would ask the manager, Susan.

"Hi Betsy," Susan smiled when she saw her. "Is everything all right today? You look a little lost."

"I feel lost," Betsy explained, "and confused, and desperate. You know what, Susan? I have decided that I am sick of living like this. I am shut away and hidden all the time. I have decided that I want one day to be allowed to explore normal human society, and I would like to take my case to court. How can this be done?"

Susan looked at Betsy in a thoughtful, understanding way. At last, she said, "Betsy, are you sure this is what you want?"

"I am sure," Betsy explained. "I've had this desire in the back of my mind for many years, maybe even my whole life, and now, I know I want to do this."

"I see," Susan replied. "Well, I don't see how, in your situation, you could afford a lawyer. I think you would be best off representing yourself. I might be wrong, but maybe self-representation could help you in your case. It might show the court how strong and sure you are in what you want; that you are willing to go through with this, even if you have to do it alone. You can apply for legal aid as well. It's a loan you can take out to help you with your case, but you will have to pay it back."

"I will," insisted Betsy. "I am willing to do anything."

"I understand," replied Susan. "I wish you luck with your case."

From that moment, the ball got rolling. Betsy composed a letter to the County of Hawaii court. After she had completed the letter, she presented it to Susan, who mailed it, via regular post, to the court's magistrate, Fred Meyer. In her mail, Betsy had included copies of the various court reports from her parents' efforts to find freedom for Betsy. On top of being smart, Betsy was a prudent girl, who had always done everything to be prepared; hence she had always carried copies of these court reports with her just in case the need arose to deliver them to any person. Then, Betsy awaited his reply. Betsy was afraid that he would laugh, would think Betsy was selfish or narcissistic, but he wrote her back with a helpful response.

Betsy Alicia Parker,

I understand how it must feel to be in your position. Your story has touched many people in your home town and the state of Hawaii. As you are an individual who is justifiably striving towards acceptance, we will set aside a court date to hear your case starting 2:00pm October 15. You will be able to take part in the hearing via video link. Please understand that it may take as long as several months for the court to come to a decision.

Justice Fred Meyer

Betsy was overjoyed when she read what Fred Meyer had to

say. With renewed enthusiasm, she downloaded the legal aid loan and applied.

Over the course of the next few weeks, she told everyone at Sunny Palms what she was doing. Some were intrigued and cheered her on. Others were unsure, and didn't think this was a wise move for Betsy. But, all in all, everyone was accepting and showed at least some support for Betsy.

Betsy had not applied to any universities or colleges, not even for video-link 'attendance.' Even if she could continue her education this way, she no longer saw any point in doing so, as she could not see what job would be able to come from it in the clothed world.

The months passed and, before Betsy knew it, October arrived, and the day arrived when she was due to begin her court case.

Betsy turned on the video link she had always used for school, and positioned herself so that only her face was visible. In the rest of the screen, Betsy saw a huge, crowded courtroom. Justice Fred Meyer's face appeared at the front of the room. Betsy was nervous. She listened for her turn to speak. The Judge was making a preliminary speech to the audience about Betsy, who she was and why she was doing this. Betsy could barely listen. She was that anxious to speak and get her voice out. Finally, the icon of the Judge moved to Betsy and asked her to tell her story.

"My name is Betsy Alicia Parker," she began, "and I will be nineteen years old in three months. In all of those years, I have yearned for understanding, love and acceptance. I ask not to be shut away for who I am, not to be treated as a threat to anyone, or to be blamed for having something that I cannot help: a condition inflicted upon me, where I had no choice in the matter. To be fair, I respect people who choose to wear clothing, as I, in part, have this very desire myself. I even respect that societal attitudes dictate that all people have to wear clothing if they're in public. But I find it hard to accept that attitude when it bars me from being a normal person. I have an allergy that forces me, against my will, to always wear the clothing I was wearing when I came out of my mother's womb: nothing at all. All my life, I have been shunned for having that allergy. Is my affliction a crime? Is my mere existence a crime? People of the court, and of the land, I ask you to consider my situation."

Several cheers sounded in the courtroom. Other people murmured. Others nodded in understanding, while a few others reacted in disgust or discomfort.

Betsy's mother was next to testify. "I honor my daughter," she began, with a smile stretching across her face. "I honor her strength, and her courage. I honor her for coming forth today to speak her voice. I have been blessed, truly blessed, to carry and give birth to this awesome young lady. Since I saw her face, for the first time, on the day she came to me and my husband Carl, I knew she was a wonderful child with a big heart. Her first word was 'love' and she loved to run and play around the back yard and play with her little sister, Laura. She adored the few other children who came over to visit her. She has shown respect and compassion for all forms of life, even the smallest of them all. In high school, she was an A student, awarded the honor roll over email. She was, and still is, so smart that she helped Laura with her homework every time Laura needed it, helping Laura to excel in her more difficult subjects. I love Betsy, I admire her, and I feel blessed and grateful to have her as my daughter."

Everyone taking the stand, who knew Betsy, testified positively on Betsy's behalf. After her mother spoke, her father took the stand. He talked about how concerned he and his wife had been when they discovered what was wrong with Betsy. Dr. Derek Crown, who was now retired, gave a speech much the same as the one he gave the news people many years ago. Then came the Nelsons, the Barnes's, Catherine and various members of Sunny Palms. There were even some students from Betsy's high school taking the stand and testifying for Betsy. Betsy waited patiently, hoping that Laura would take the stand, but Laura never showed her face, ever.

There were people raising a case against Betsy. Some were sympathetic, but argued that the rights of many people not to see Betsy trumped the right of one person, Betsy herself, to be allowed to go out; that it would cause too much discomfort, awkwardness, and that it wouldn't be suitable for children to be around if Betsy was granted the right, however brief, to have the same rights as any other person. Others were vehemently against Betsy. They branded her as nothing more than a sick young woman who wanted nothing more than to draw attention to herself.

Then, there came a period of cross examination, in which peoples' viewpoints were argued back and forth. Betsy's family argued against the 'needs-of-the-many' argument by explaining that Betsy's entire life had been awkward and restricted. If Betsy was granted a day in human society, then any offence a person might feel at the sight of Betsy would be trivial in comparison to the hiding and shunning that Betsy had had to endure for close to nineteen years.

Others argued against Betsy and her family by saying that Betsy being allowed to go out could start a great bout of ordinary people wanting the same right as her. A great wave of indecent exposure cases could result, stemming from a ruling in favor of Betsy.

Betsy and her family countered that the existence of the nudist lifestyle, and advocacy for it, had not sparked a long string of the general population wanting to bare their bodies in public. Therefore, such an outcome was unlikely if Betsy won.

At the end of the cross-examination period, the Judge announced, "Now that all witnesses have been called, and the public's opinions have been cast, I shall deliberate what the outcome shall be. For the time being, I dismiss all parties involved."

The parties of the case departed, and Betsy turned off the video link.

"How do you feel about the case?" Catherine asked Betsy later that day.

"I don't know," Betsy replied. "I feel there were a lot of good points made and good arguments raised. To tell the truth, it is awfully tedious wearing no clothes all the time. It makes me feel like an animal. But I suppose, biologically, that is what I am."

"You are absolutely right about that. Betsy, whatever happens, I am glad to have you as a friend."

"And I'm glad to have you," Betsy smiled. "I am prepared to lose. If the court rules that I must not stray beyond home and the nudist world, I will understand and accept that; although I won't be able to help feeling a little disappointed."

"I can see that," acknowledged Catherine. "Whatever Justice Meyer rules, I know you did your best."

"And I know that too, and I think, in the long run, that will be reward enough."

***

In the middle of January, on Betsy's nineteenth birthday to be exact, she received the following letter.

Betsy Alicia Parker,

I, Justice Fred Meyer, have deliberated both sides of the case thoroughly. I have weighed the pros and cons and recognize that your needs and society's needs are both relevant. As such, the County of Hawaii has granted a writ that shall allow you to have one day of immunity against indecent exposure charges so that you may have a chance to explore human society. On all of Saturday, January 22, from midnight at the start of that day until midnight at the end of that day, you may venture wherever you want to, but you must maintain casual, conformist behavior and behave no differently than if you were clothed. There will be a press release going out so that the public will be alerted to your presence. By the end of this day, you must retreat back to Sunny Palms. I wish you the best of luck.

Justice Fred Meyer

"YES!!!" Betsy screamed after she had read the letter. "Catherine! Look at this! This is wonderful! We did it! We really really did it!"

"Betsy," Catherine smiled back. "I am so happy for you. Congratulations on getting your day of acceptance in human society. You really earned it."

"For just one day at last," Betsy beamed, not truly believing this was happening, "I get to be accepted as an actual human being. This is the best birthday present I have ever had."

15 A Happy Meeting

Betsy was overjoyed for the time being, but as the week wore on, she began to develop reservations. Although it would be legal for Betsy to go out in public that one day, she was nervous about how the public would react. If even one person looked away, or stared at her for too long, Betsy would feel like she was putting herself on display, and she would feel like a fool for making the court grant her this right.

On the other hand, Betsy was too excited to let these reservations get the better of her. On the evening of January 21, she turned to Catherine and said "good night."

"Will you get up at midnight?" Catherine asked in return. "Will you make your way out of Sunny Palms right when the clock strikes twelve, and begin your gadabout in civilization? This is going to be a special day and you won't want to waste a minute of it."

"Oh no," Betsy replied. "I need my sleep. I will head out first thing tomorrow morning, and see where the day takes me."

Betsy lay in her waterbed, and in a few minutes was fast asleep.

At 7:00 the next morning, Betsy awoke. She stood up, ate breakfast, showered, let the sun dry her, and headed out into the morning.

"Hey Betsy!" Catherine called. "I will come with you. I will be dressed, of course, but I want you to have at least one friend with you, to keep you company, and keep an eye out for you in case something goes awry. I'll pack your silicon pad too."

"Thank you Catherine," Betsy smiled. "I appreciate your thoughtfulness and understanding. We can look out for each other."

As they were heading out, Betsy and Catherine stopped by

Susan's office.

"Good morning Susan," Betsy smiled. "I am going out to explore the world."

"Have a good day, Betsy," Susan beamed from her desk. "I will see you tonight."

Susan opened the gate for Betsy, and Betsy headed out.

The feeling that came over Betsy as she headed out the gate, onto the road, was the most bizarre sensation Betsy had ever experienced. She felt a sudden sense of shyness and vulnerability. Betsy turned to Catherine, and felt a sense of relief come over her, as she saw her faithful companion at her side.

"Where do you want to go, Betsy?" Catherine asked. "You don't want to go about wandering aimlessly in your birthday suit."

"There's a coffee shop about half-an-hour's walk from here," Betsy explained, "called Fresh Cafe. Why don't we make a stop there?"

"That sounds perfect," Catherine beamed. "Let's grab some coffee."

As Betsy and Catherine walked along, they did meet a few people on the roadside. In general, these people passed Betsy and Catherine by as though Betsy and Catherine were ordinary people. A few others smiled at Betsy and waved, obviously pleased with the fact that Betsy was allowed in the open at last. There were some others who waved their hands and cheered.

Betsy didn't like it when people did this. She wasn't sure whether they meant well or whether they were mocking her, but Betsy did not like the excessive attention either way.

"Hey," Betsy would tell them. "I'm just a person, nothing more. You don't give that much attention to people, do you?"

These people would then look apologetic and walk away.

When Betsy and Catherine came into the area with houses,

buildings and shops, Betsy's nervousness peaked, and she began trembling.

“It's okay, Betsy,” Catherine soothed. “Look, we'll be at Fresh Cafe very soon.”

Even in the populated area, most people payed little to no attention to Betsy, much to her relief. There were a few men who stared at her, but Betsy and Catherine stared at them back, which drove these men away in humiliation.

At last, they reached Fresh Cafe, and Catherine held the door open for her friend.

“Here you go, Betsy,” Catherine smiled. Betsy stepped inside, and Catherine followed.

It was a quaint little shop. It had a counter with a wide selection of scones, omelettes and rolls. Although it was early in the day, Betsy noticed one other customer, a teenage boy, sitting alone at a table.

Still nervous at showing herself to the worker behind the counter, Betsy ordered some coffee and a scone. Catherine ordered the same and paid for both herself and Betsy. The man working at the counter served Betsy and Catherine their food as though they were regular customers. The girls thanked the man, then walked to the nearest table.

“I think I'll eat with this young man here,” Betsy explained to Catherine. “He looks lonely.”

Betsy took her coffee and scone, put her pad down on the seat beside the boy, and sat down at the table next to him. He looked up from his food and beverage to face Betsy.

“You must be Betsy Parker,” he smiled. “You have been in the news a lot. I suspect everyone in the states might know about you by now. Congratulations on winning that case by the way.”

Betsy didn't know how to respond. She wasn't sure whether

she should take this as forced attention, or if he was only wanting to be friendly.

"I am Betsy," she replied. "How are you doing today?"

"I'm fine, still a bit tired. I often come to this coffee shop in the morning to help myself wake up for school, except, on Saturdays I tutor math to an eighth grade student at his house. His name is Keith Reynolds and he's finding it easier and more fun, now that I'm helping him. I'm in twelfth grade."

"Good for you," Betsy smiled. "It's good that you're volunteering your time to help another student. Do you know what you are planning to become?"

"Something I have always wanted to be is a teacher. I took up tutoring because it's quite a bit like that. When I graduate from high school at the end of this year, I would like to find a proper job."

"I graduated from high school last summer," Betsy explained, "only it wasn't much of a graduation. I did really well in school, but I had to watch my classes over video, and stay home from the grad celebrations. I guess I'm at least getting somewhere."

"I think you are too," the young man smiled. "My name is Mark by the way, Mark Turner."

"Pleased to meet you Mark," Betsy smiled.

Then, Betsy thought, that with Catherine here, she might as well introduce her friend. "This is Catherine," explained Betsy. "She has taken up residence at Sunny Palms nudist resort with me. I've been friends with her since I met her there when we were both little girls."

"It's good to see that you have made a friend," Mark smiled. Then, he continued, "So, Betsy. What do you plan to do with your life?"

Betsy sighed, and thought. "I don't know. I'm still puzzling over that. The one thing I have always wanted to be is a nurse. I would love to have a job, like that, that focusses on helping other people, but I can't see how that's possible."

"You could find a job at Sunny Palms," Mark suggested.

"I suppose you're right," Betsy replied, "but I don't want to work only for other nudists. I want to work for and help all people."

"Well," sighed Mark. "There are some times when you just can't get what you want, and you have to live with it whether you like it or not."

"You've had an experience where you couldn't get what you wanted?"

"You bet," explained Mark, "All my life. I've grown up in a household raised by very strict, rigid parents. They are the kinds of people who would be very much against someone like you. In fact, I just know that I would be in big trouble if they ever found out I even spoke to you."

"I'm so sorry to hear that," said Betsy. "Unfortunately, I have had people like that come and go in my own life. Over time, I have learned to ignore it and move on."

"But it's harder when those people are your parents," Mark continued. "Up till I was about ten years old, I didn't even question them. I took for granted, and followed through with all their teachings and their beliefs. After all, they were, and are, my parents, my caregivers, and therefore they ought to know best.

"But when you, Betsy, became more prominent in the news and media, I thought 'Wow, this young lady is so outgoing and strong, and she continues to stand up for what she believes in, even though she can't wear clothes.' I then began to question my upbringing and my parents, and I have come to decide they are wrong."

"Did you ever tell them your feelings?" Betsy asked.

Mark shook his head. "There would be no use. I would be in

huge trouble. I might even get disowned."

"Are you in a position where you could move out?"

"Not quite yet," Mark explained. "I turned eighteen a week ago, but I'm still in high school, and don't have a job, except for my tutoring. Until I get a proper job and education, I will be forced to live under my parents' roof."

"Well, I hope you can move out soon," replied Betsy, "so that you can make your own way, free of how your parents want you to live."

Mark decided to change the subject. "So how do you like human society, Betsy?"

"I like it," Betsy smiled. "It's fascinating. I am happy to see that most people are reacting as if I'm a normal person. I have met a few people of the undesirable sort, but I guess that's to be expected."

"That's their problem, not yours," Mark explained. "Betsy," he continued, looking her in the eyes. "I don't think you're weird."

"Thank you," Betsy smiled. "I don't think so either. In fact, I know I'm not, even if not everyone agrees with that."

For the rest of their time at Fresh Cafe, neither Betsy nor Mark said another word. They drank their coffee and ate their breakfasts. Then, Mark stood up to leave.

"I have to go to Keith's house now," he explained. "It was wonderful to meet you, Betsy. I would love to talk to you again."

"You can reach me at Sunny Palms," Betsy explained. Mark handed Betsy two pieces of paper, and they copied down each other's phone numbers. Betsy wrote Sunny Palms' number and gave it to Mark. Mark wrote down his home phone number, and cellphone number, and gave them to Betsy.

"Bye Betsy!" Mark called as he headed out the door.

"Bye Mark!" Betsy called. "Have a good tutoring session!"

"I'm sure I will," he smiled, and left the coffee shop.

After Betsy and Catherine had left, they took a walk down the road, out into a patch of woods. By now, the sun was well above the horizon and the grass was shiny and golden. The air and sun felt warm on Betsy.

"This is so amazing," Betsy smiled at Catherine. "I have never felt anything like this before, ever. I wish this day could last forever."

"It could if you allow it to," Catherine replied in contentment and awe. "Just look at the Hau Willow over there."

It was a gorgeous tree, with its leaves swaying in the breeze. An ant crawled down its trunk.

"My mother's maiden name was Willow," Betsy beamed. "It's such a gorgeous name. I wish she had kept it."

"Say, Betsy?" asked Catherine. "You think you'll ever get married?"

"Me? No, I don't think so. Not that I don't want to. It would be lovely, but I don't think I would ever get a chance to meet someone meaningful enough."

"Would you take his name if you did?" asked Catherine.

Betsy shook her head. "No, I'd rather my mother had kept hers, so I think I'll keep mine. Willow sounds much better than Parker, but, who knows? If I change my name I might come to regret it; you know; miss my name."

"So would I," Catherine agreed.

Then, Betsy's mellow smile grew into a happy playful smile, then into a laugh.

"Hey Catherine!" she called. "Let's play some tag. We're out in an open field, and I feel like a kid once again!"

"All right!" Catherine grinned. "I'm set if you are."

With a refreshed smile across Betsy's face, and a renewed sense of enthusiasm, Betsy ran across the field, starting out as 'it' to tag Catherine. Catherine ran, in a playful, merry sprint. Betsy caught up to Catherine and tagged her. Catherine gave a scream of delight and turned around to pursue Betsy. After a wild, rigorous play, Catherine collapsed into the grass, laughing.

"Oh Betsy!" she cried. "You've got such joy and enthusiasm."

Betsy decided that she had had enough playing too, as her run slowed into a walk, and she stopped running altogether. "That felt great!" she cried. "I felt like my real self with that game of tag just now. I wish I could live like that forever."

"What do you want to do now Betsy?" Catherine asked.

"I have had enough of being out. Let's go back to Sunny Palms."

"But we've only been out for a couple hours and we've got most of the day ahead of us. Betsy, this is such a unique, special day for you. You'll probably never get one like this ever again."

"I know," Betsy replied, "but I don't see anything more I can do that's useful. Come on; let's go back."

"All right Betsy," Catherine sighed, "if that's really what you want."

And so, Betsy and Catherine turned and walked back to Sunny Palms, the one, and only place where Betsy was welcome.

16 Mark's Adventure

When Betsy awoke the next morning, she half-thought that her adventure the day before had been a dream. Nonetheless, she knew, in her heart and soul, that the previous day had been as real as any other, and now it was over. Betsy had to return to her normal, sheltered life.

As she rose to her feet, she felt a deep sense of regret. The fact had now sunk in that she could have spent the full twenty-four hours of the previous day getting to know people, settling in, at least trying to become a part of the actual human world. But Betsy had spent only about two hours of that day in the human world, and in those two hours, she had met only one other person. Now she knew, that she had failed. She would never get an opportunity like this ever again, and she had wasted this one chance she had. If only Betsy had listened to Catherine, when Catherine suggested that Betsy stay in the public domain all day, to at least get to meet more people, more fully, and do more.

But do what? Not even Betsy knew. And here she was, alone, on this desert island called "Sunny Palms" a prison, where Betsy was locked away forever for a crime she had never committed.

Would she ever see Mark again? He seemed like such a friendly, understanding young man, who had courage enough to question his own upbringing. The more Betsy thought about Mark, the more she burned to see him one more time. He was the first, and only, adult person in the human world, who was not family, who truly understood and accepted Betsy. For this, Betsy was grateful. She had met someone. At least, that was a start. But where would the path lead from that start? Betsy had to know. She did the first and most obvious thing she could think of, which was to turn to

Catherine.

"Catherine," Betsy called. "I feel so exhilarated from yesterday, but so lost as well. I really liked meeting Mark in that coffee shop yesterday, and I've got to see him one more time."

"Well Betsy," replied Catherine. "You have his phone number."

"I know I do," breathed Betsy, "but I don't want to get him into any trouble with his parents. I only got to meet Mark for maybe ten minutes, then he had to leave, and he was so caring and understanding towards me."

"Call him if you like, if you think it's worth the risk," replied Catherine. "It's your decision, not mine."

"I know, Catherine, but it's not that simple. What if I call and one of his parents answers the phone? They will ask who I am, and why I'm calling."

"Betsy, he gave you his cellphone number yesterday. I'm pretty sure his parents are not going to answer their son's cellphone."

"I guess you're right, but what if, while I'm talking to him, his parents overhear and figure out what's going on?"

"Betsy, the guy's eighteen. Even if they're so strict towards him, I very much doubt that, at his age, they would be so concerned for him that they would resort to nosiness to find out what's going on."

Betsy spent the long hours of that day thinking about what to do. She went for a swim in her pool. She went for a walk around the grounds. She went for a walk in the woods. She sat on her silicon bed, thinking.

Finally, it was ten o'clock at night, and Betsy still had not called Mark. She was so desperate. She picked up her phone and dialled his number.

"Hello," came Mark's voice from the other end.

"Hi, this is Betsy. We met at Fresh Cafe, and we spoke briefly in the coffee shop."

"Hello Betsy; I remember you. How did your day go?"

"I didn't exactly do much. After walking and enjoying some time with Catherine, I decided there was nothing more for me to do, so I went home."

"Oh Betsy, you had the whole day to do things, and you wasted most of it."

"I know. Please don't rub it in. It's just that I had met you and gone for a walk with my friend. What more could I have done anyway?"

"I'm sorry," replied Mark. "I guess you're right, but anyway, what brings you on the phone?"

"Mark," Betsy sighed, mustering her courage. The plan Betsy had in mind was risky, but she had to get it out to Mark if she had any hope of seeing him again. "I cannot come out to see you. The law doesn't allow me to, but, I was wondering, do you think there is any way you could come out to see me? I live at Sunny Palms nudist resort."

"Well," sighed Mark. "My parents wouldn't allow it. That's for sure. If I ever come to Sunny Palms, I will have to do it in some way my parents don't know. How about, tomorrow, I call in sick from school, and, instead of going to school, I come out to Sunny Palms, while my parents think I'm in school. I can stay just for the morning and afternoon. Then, I can come home at the same time the school day ends, so that my parents don't suspect anything."

Betsy thought about Mark's proposition. She didn't like it. Mark would be lying to his school and deceiving his parents, and Betsy would be responsible for all of it. Mark would miss a day of school, too, which would put him behind. Worse still, was that it was a plan not even guaranteed to succeed, that Mark's parents might find out and he'd be in big trouble, and Betsy would be left feeling like his punishment was her fault.

"Mark," Betsy explained, "You don't have to miss school. You could tell your parents, one evening, that you're going to study with some friends, or that you're going to the movies. When you do go out, you could come to see me instead." Betsy didn't like that idea either because Mark would still be lying, but at least it would be better than him missing a day of school, and therefore lying, not only to his parents, but to his school as well.

"Betsy," Mark explained, "If only you knew my parents, you would not be suggesting that. My parents have very strict rules requiring me to stay at home every night to do my homework. I can see my friends all I want while I'm at school, but once I'm at home, my parents limit my social interactions to one hour per night, for any reason, whether it's studying, socializing, doing fun activities or anything at all. There would be no way I would be able to come out to see you, have a proper visit with you, and come home all within an hour. If I even tried that, my parents would know, right away, that something was amiss."

Betsy spent the next minute thinking of something else that could be done, a plan which would allow her to see Mark that wasn't so risky or deceptive. Alas, she could think of nothing.

Betsy sighed, "All right. I guess your idea works. I will see you, tomorrow, at Sunny Palms then."

"Well!" Mark cried, in a happy and thankful voice. "It was nice talking to you. I will see you tomorrow. Bye for now."

He and Betsy hung up.

By sheer luck, Susan walked past where Betsy had been talking on the phone, heading to her campsite to get ready for bed.

"Susan," Betsy called. "Can I have a quick word?"

"Sure you may, Betsy," Susan beamed. "Any time."

"I made a friend yesterday when I was exploring society. His name is Mark Turner and he would like to come here tomorrow morning and afternoon for a quick visit. Is that all right with you?"

"You found a friend yesterday?" cried Susan. "That's wonderful! Well, I'm so glad you had a good day in human society yesterday. You sure earned it. Of course it's fine if you bring Mark into the grounds tomorrow. Why don't you come to the office at the time you'll be expecting him to come around and you can help show him the grounds?"

"I will," Betsy beamed. "I look forward to seeing Mark."

***

When Mark awoke the next morning, he packed his backpack and made his breakfast (toast, bacon and eggs) as calmly as he could. He wanted to make sure he behaved as normally as possible. As soon as Mark left the house, he turned on his cellphone and called the school.

"H ... hell ... o," Mark gasped in a coughing, raspy voice. "Is this ... the prin (cough) (cough) cipal?"

"Yes it is," came the respondent's voice. "Who are you? Are you okay?"

"I am Mark (cough) Turner," he continued in his raspy voice. "I am really ... sick ... today. I have a (cough) fever, and a really sore ... throat."

"Oh dear," came the voice of the principal. "You sure sound sick. I will mark you as absent for today. Please get some rest. I hope you get better soon."

"Thank ... you. I (cough) (cough) hope so (cough) too."

Mark turned the phone off.

As Mark walked down the driveway, he stopped, looked at his

car, which his parents had bought for him as an eighteenth birthday present, and thought, "Maybe I should drive over. It will be much quicker than walking, and I want to spend as much time with Betsy as I can."

However, as quickly as the thought had entered his head, Mark decided against it. Mark walked to school every day, and he didn't want to do anything out of the ordinary, for fear that it might make his parents suspicious. Mark decided that he would walk to Sunny Palms.

Mark knew how to get to Sunny Palms. He had the coordinates set on his GPS. It wouldn't be much of a walk. After all, he lived a reasonable walking distance from Fresh Cafe, and, since Betsy had come to Fresh Cafe on her walk, so did Betsy. Therefore, it couldn't take all that much longer to walk to Sunny Palms, despite the apparent fact that neither of Mark's parents knew the place existed at all.

Mark headed down the road, his GPS in his hands, guiding his way. He felt a combination of rebelliousness, that he was going against his oppressive parents to do what he wanted, excitement at seeing Betsy, nervousness, as he had never been to a nudist resort before, and a tinge of guilt that he was lying to his parents and to the school.

As he strode along, the nervousness was really getting to him. His parents were so stringent that they hadn't even enrolled him in gym class in school. They didn't want him to be naked around others for any reason, and that included the locker room. He did own a bathing suit, but his parents only allowed him to use it in their pool and hot tub at home.

Nonetheless, Mark was determined. He kept the thought of Betsy in his mind, and this was the light that kept him going. He was going to see Betsy, and hopefully meet many other happy people, and do many fun things.

When Mark arrived, Susan was already at the gate to greet him.

"I'm Mark," he explained, "Mark Turner. I'm Betsy's new friend."

"Well yes, Betsy has told me all about you. Please come on in. I am Susan, the manager."

She opened the gate and Mark stepped inside.

"I'm only staying for the afternoon, so I don't need accommodation," Mark explained.

"I know," replied Susan. "Betsy has let me know."

As soon as Mark stepped into the general portion of the grounds, Betsy caught sight of him and hurried to meet him.

"You're here Mark!" she cried. "Isn't it lovely?"

"This is so strange," Mark stuttered. "I don't know where to look."

"Just look like you normally would," Betsy replied. "Naturally, that's what I've done my whole life. Every sight in nature is just as pretty as any other, and people are a part of nature too."

"I guess that makes sense," Mark said. "I think I'll stay dressed though. I feel awkward enough as it is, and I don't want to step any more out of line than I already am."

"Very well, if that's what you want," replied Betsy. "Where do you want to go first, Mark?"

"To the pool. It's such a hot day, and I'm craving a cool swim. I packed my bathing suit, because I'd feel too weird undressed. I only came out here to see you, not get naked."

"No bathing suits are allowed in the pool," Betsy explained. "That's a rule at pretty well any nudist club or resort."

"No bathing suits? Oh!" he cried. "Well, I guess that leaves me with no choice."

Mark removed his shirt. Then, he put his thumbs under his

shorts and underwear, and made a struggling sort of expression.

"NO!" Mark cried at last. "NO! I can't do it!"

To be honest, Mark felt sheepish and silly inside. Here he was, standing beside this girl, whom he was just getting to know as a friend, who had spent her entire life naked, because she had an allergic condition that forced her to live a clothes-free life, and here he was, wanting to respect her, wanting to become her friend, but he was unable to force himself into a state of being that she had taken for granted her entire life. Mark turned to face Betsy once more.

"Does it humiliate you?" he asked. "Is your life one big, endless, continuous embarrassment, having to live like that?"

"No," Betsy replied. "This is what I'm used to, as it is all I have ever known. It is awkward though," she admitted, "and inconvenient. I feel no shame, no self-consciousness, no embarrassment, but a lot of the time I feel even worse off than the disabled people of this planet: the blind, the deaf, those with mental or physical impairments. At least they have respect, care and compassion from society. They can take comfort in knowing that there are other people like them, and that they're not alone, not alone because they're cared for and not alone because there are others who also have their affliction. But me, I am truly alone. There is no one else on Earth who has my affliction, and most people are so absorbed in thinking that nakedness is indecent that they don't give a hoot about me. I feel like a stranger, a ghost, bound to the face of the Earth, hearing of so many people living successful, happy lives, while I am always shut out, alone, even though I can see, hear and use my body perfectly well."

"Oh Betsy," Mark answered. "I am so sorry. I understand how hard everything must be for you. I fully respect your choice to take your issue to court to have one day to be yourself. If I had been in your shoes, I'd have probably tried to sway a court to make my *entire* life like that."

Mark struggled once more, and with shaking hands, and a sweaty face, he managed to disrobe.

"DON'T LOOK AT ME!!!" Mark hollered when he was down to his bare skin.

A few other people around jerked their heads towards Mark, startled.

"Oh God!" Mark cried, clasping his hands down to cover his genitals. "I can't believe I just did that. I feel like a criminal."

Betsy made a warm, sympathetic smile. "Good for you for trying," she soothed. "Look, we can take a quick dip in the pool. As long as you stay underwater, you won't be easily visible."

"You think?" Mark stuttered. "What if some weird voyeur bobs underwater to take a look at me?"

"Mark," Betsy reassured him. "Nobody is going to do that. The people here are not like that. For eleven years before I came to live here, my family frequently brought me to this place, so I could have a chance to live the way I am and be accepted. In all that time, not one person has done any such thing to me or to anyone else."

"Take me to the pool then," Mark stammered.

Mark and Betsy passed by the usual chlorinated pool, and Betsy stopped him at the un-chlorinated little pool the managers had set up for her, when she first came to Sunny Palms.

"This pool is made specially for me," Betsy explained. "It has no chlorine in it, so that I can swim in it without my skin reacting to it. The managers have taught me how to keep it clean. I drain and refill it every day, like a bathtub, and they clean it out once a week, so that the water doesn't get dirty."

"I see," Mark replied. "I understand how it would get dirty quickly."

Mark stepped into the water quickly, in a hurry to hide his

body.

"There," he breathed. "That feels better ... I think."

Betsy and Mark spent the next five minutes soaking in the water, listening to the birdsong, feeling the breeze, before Mark spoke up once more.

"So?" he asked. "Do you see anything of your family anymore?"

"I see my parents from time to time," Betsy replied. "They last came here at the end of December to visit me at Christmas time."

"You have any brothers or sisters?"

"I have one younger sister, Laura," Betsy explained. "She'll be sixteen in February. There's nothing wrong with her skin, or anything else about her, except" Betsy paused, "she has grown away from me. She doesn't feel comfortable being around me anymore, and that's why I have moved here to stay. It's kind of funny really. She used to come here with me and our parents, and she once enjoyed it, but now she finds it embarrassing and uncomfortable. Just before I left my parents' home to live here, Laura said that she's not even sure she'll come out and visit me. So far she hasn't, and I don't know if I'll ever see her again."

"Yes, I understand. That's tough," Mark commented, "but she's sixteen, pretty much. I bet she feels her reputation is at stake, so she feels like she has to distance herself from you."

"Do you have any brothers or sisters Mark?" Betsy asked.

"I am the younger of two brothers," Mark explained. "My older brother, Roger, is a chip off the old block from my parents. He's five years older than me, and he's moved out now, and to tell you the truth, the day he moved out, and ever since, I felt it was good riddance. He's selfish, cold, unfeeling, rigid, and I daresay, downright cruel. A bully, to put it simply."

"I'm so sorry Mark," sighed Betsy. "I thought I was having a hard time with Laura, but it sounds like your brother takes the cake."

"Believe me Betsy," continued Mark, "compared to Roger, your sister is an angel. You miss Laura, but I rejoice at not having to see Roger. To make matters worse, Roger was always my parents' favorite child. Every hard, cruel lesson they taught, Roger absorbed it hook, line and sinker. He never thought for himself, never questioned his upbringing, not once. My parents spoiled Roger rotten, calling it 'rewards for his good behavior.' Roger would kill me if he knew I was here, and would kill me twice more if he found out I was talking to you, as would my parents for that matter."

"What's Roger doing, now that he's moved out?"

"He's got a wife, Rochelle," Mark explained, "and they have a two-year-old son, Xavier. I only hope and pray Xavier doesn't grow up to be like Roger and my parents. I saw their son a month ago, when Roger and Rochelle came over at Christmas, and he's such a delightful, spunky little boy. It would be a terrible shame if he got turned into something like his father and grandparents."

Betsy decided to change the subject.

"Look," she smiled, "it's a lovely day. It's so peaceful here. Can't we just be happy for a while?"

"I suppose," Mark replied, "but isn't there a quieter place we can be? There's too many people around here, and I feel overexposed."

"We can go to the sauna," suggested Betsy. "It's much quieter there, and there's usually little to no people inside."

"You're on," Mark replied. "Let's go."

Betsy and Mark left the pool, and walked over to the sauna. They stepped inside and closed the door behind them.

"Whoo this is hot!" Mark called as soon as they were inside.

Much to Mark's relief, there was nobody else inside the sauna.

"This is much quieter," Mark breathed in relief. "If only I

could stay here forever for just a bit of privacy."

Betsy wished that Mark could be content, just for the six hours that he was away from school, but she knew that wasn't going to happen. Betsy just sat on her silicon pad, happy to be with Mark, happy that she was helping him to come out of his life of torment.

He was definitely on his way, Betsy thought. He already respected her enough to skip school to see her, to listen to the story of her life and be interested, and tell her everything about his own life. Maybe, Betsy thought, just maybe, give it some time, and he would become a close, true friend, as happy and free to be naked, as she was. Of course, she would still think Mark was an awesome guy if he didn't. She would still like him, but maybe, he might yet take the final step of shedding his inhibitions.

Betsy's attention was drawn away by Mark sniffing the air. When Betsy thought about it, she realized that there was a burning smell. The sauna seemed to have grown hotter as well.

Then, all within a split second, a flame shot up from a board near the floor, licked Mark's leg, made Mark scream, and the board fell crashing down, in flames, into Mark, scorching his abdomen, and Mark yelled in pain and fright.

He and Betsy yanked the door open and hurried out of the sauna, but Mark was already badly burned.

"The sauna's on fire!" Mark hollered, and collapsed onto the ground, unable to move any further.

A nearby man called 911 on his cellphone.

As Mark was sprawled on the ground, Betsy grabbed hold of his hands and pulled him away from the burning sauna.

"Mark," Betsy cried, when they were a safe distance away, "I'm so sorry Mark. I shouldn't have suggested we go to the sauna."

"It's all right," Mark gasped. "You didn't know it was going to catch fire."

Mark and Betsy looked back at the sauna, which was, by now, nothing more than a huge ball of flames. Mark lay on the ground, staring in fear and worry at the burning sauna. He looked at his leg and chest, which were dark red and crusty. "The secret's out," he stuttered. "What am I going to tell my parents?"

Betsy didn't answer. She didn't know what to answer, and Mark wasn't expecting an answer. It was a rhetorical question, expressing his own fear and horror at the situation. He was in big trouble. He knew it. It was inevitable and there was no way out.

A few minutes later, a fire truck pulled through the gate. They pulled out a hose, and sprayed the sauna until all the flames had been put out. An ambulance arrived and loaded Mark onto a stretcher.

"Take me!" Betsy cried to the paramedics. "He's my friend. I must see him in the hospital."

"You are not fit to go to the hospital, unless you, yourself, are in critical danger," one of them instructed. "We do apologize, but that's the way things are."

The paramedics whisked Mark away, leaving Betsy behind in tears.

17 A Rude Awakening

Mark awoke in the hospital, to find himself lying in bed, wearing a gown. His right leg was aching and burning, and even with the drugs the medical staff had provided, Mark felt like the pain would never go away.

"You have visitors sir," a nearby doctor told Mark.

"Betsy?" Mark thought, "Could it be her? Please let it be Betsy."

He knew it was a silly thought. The hospital staff would never let Betsy into the hospital, and she'd probably get arrested on the street if she even tried to walk to the hospital. But Mark was aching to see Betsy. Despite the fact that he knew, to his core, that Betsy couldn't possibly be here, Mark had a faint, desperate hope that maybe, just maybe, it was her.

Mark turned onto his side to see who had come to keep him company.

"Oh no!" he groaned out loud. There, by his bedside, were his parents.

"What happened to you?" cried his mother. "You had better have a solid explanation for this, young man."

Mark's mind reeled. He didn't know what to say. He couldn't say anything about Betsy, about Sunny Palms, or about being naked. He would be in the worst trouble. Mark thought of the most plausible sounding story he could think of.

"It happened at school," he began, "we were in chemistry class. We were heating some (Mark looked around the hospital room, and caught sight of some milk of magnesia that was being administered to the patient adjacent from Mark) milk of magnesia over a bunsen burner. I dropped my beaker on my foot. It caught fire, and the fire spread all the way up my leg. And now, here I am."

"Oh really?" inquired his father. "That sounds rather far-fetched, but we will call your chemistry teacher to see how real this is."

"It's real," Mark insisted. "Just as real as this hospital around you. There's no need to call the school. That's really how I got burned."

"Well, we'll just make sure," Mr. Turner insisted.

Mark's father called the school.

"Hello?" ... "Called in sick? No, Mark left home today and went to school." ... "What do you mean he didn't come to school? He wasn't sick. We saw him as he headed out the door and he was perfectly fine." ... "What's that you suggest? He skipped?" ... "Okay, well I'll talk to him about this. Thank you for clearing this up."

Mark's father hung up the phone. "Young man?!" he growled at his son. "What's this I hear about you calling in sick? Did you pretend to be sick so that you could skip school and go off someplace else?"

"Well," ... Mark paused. The truth was going to cost him everything. He fumbled for the right words to minimize the reaction from his father. "Okay, I did, but it's no big deal. I didn't go anywhere real special."

"Where did you go?" his father demanded, "and no lying about it."

"Hey, I'm all sick and bandaged up," Mark protested. "Can't we give this a rest until I get better?"

"Where did you go?" Mr. Turner repeated more sternly.

"If you must know, I went to the movies. 'The Actor Does a Trick' had just come out and I had to go see it."

"'The Actor Does a Trick?' That came out four years ago."

"Well, I'm all burned up, and I'm dopey. My memory, for

dates right now, is not so good."

By now, both of Mark's parents were furious. They were determined to get to the bottom of this. Mark could tell. They didn't even care that their son was injured. All they cared about was the truth for why he had lied about being sick so that he could skip school, and they wouldn't shut up until they found out the truth, once and for all.

"Why did you miss school today?" persisted his parents. "What were you doing?"

Mark sighed. He was cornered now. There was no way out. He would have to tell them about Betsy and the nudist resort. Mark knew it was in vain, but deep down, he hoped and prayed they would at least be gracious enough to have sympathy for Betsy, and see reason.

"Okay okay, I'll tell you," Mark sighed, whilst shaking in fear of what his parents' reaction was going to be, and sweating all the while, "I went to see Betsy Parker. She's that girl who's been in the news a lot, the one that recently won that writ to have a day nude in human society. While she was having her walk that day, she met me in Fresh Cafe. We had a lovely talk. She's a wonderful person. She really is. She invited me to come for a stay, with her, at Sunny Palms, so I did. That's what I was doing when you thought I was in school. I got burned because we went to the sauna and it caught fire. Betsy has been through so much. Please have the grace to at least understand her, and go easy on me since I told the truth."

The expressions on Mark's parents turned from impatience to disgust, and from disgust to outright horror.

"You did what?!" exclaimed his mother at last.

"I'm sorry," Mark cried. "I know I shouldn't have, but Betsy really wanted to see me, and I really wanted to see her, and she-"

"You disobedient brat of a son," his father stammered. "You

hear me now. You are never ever ever to set foot anywhere near Betsy Parker ever again. You hear me?!"

"Father!" Mark cried. "Please have a heart. She's not who you think she is. She's so kind to everyone. She's smart too. She got A's all through high school, despite the fact she could never attend any of her classes. She's a really pleasant, sweet, fun girl. She's lost and confused, and all she wants is to be loved."

"She is a sick exhibitionist, possessed by the devil!" barked Mr. Turner shortly.

"She's a person, just like you and me, and she needs respect!" Mark insisted.

"Not a person!" Mark's father cried. "One of the defining characteristics of a person is that a person can wear clothing to keep itself decent. Since Betsy lacks that characteristic, you are to treat her for what she is; an animal."

"But father!"

"God would NEVER create a 'person' that has to be an exhibitionist in order to live. I tell you, she is of the devil Mark. She is a beast, and you are to have no affiliation with her."

"But she can't even get a job!"

"Sure she can get a job," Mrs. Turner cried out, "as a porn star!"

At that utterance, a volcano exploded inside Mark. "THAT DOES IT!" Mark yelled. "YOU TWO ARE CLEARING OUT OF MY HOSPITAL ROOM NOW. YOU'RE JUST AS BAD AS ROGER, BOTH OF YOU!"

"Roger actually had respect for his parents!" Mr. Turner yelled, "and he still does, unlike the way you're turning out to be."

"I have no regrets about going to see Betsy," cried Mark. "In fact, I'm glad I did. And I will gladly see her again, and again, and maybe even stay with her forever, stay by her side, and never leave her, no matter what. And so help me if you stand in my way."

"See her again and again?" gasped his father. "Mark, what sort of depravity is this? So you want to see this naked girl every day, do you? You lust after her, Mark. She's so attractive and so pretty with all her clothes off, that you can't get enough of looking at her. Well I'm telling you, that you can cut this out right now, and never see her again!"

"It's not like that!" Mark yelled. "I like BETSY. I don't like her beauty; I don't like her nakedness. I like HER, her personality, her heart, her individuality, her SELF. Betsy Parker could turn into a hideous beast, and I wouldn't care. I'd stick with her, because she'd be the exact same person on the inside. Betsy could get over her allergy, and become able to wear clothing and function like everyone else, but she would still be HER, I would like her no less, and I wouldn't dream of leaving her. In fact, I'd be happy for her."

"So," growled Mr. Turner, "if Betsy had been normal, or had been a hideous beast, when you met her for the first time, would you be raving about her like you are right now? Don't lie to me boy! I don't think so!"

"What attracted me to Betsy was her courage!" Mark insisted, "her strength and stamina to live life like a normal person. That courage of hers was what inspired me to feel the compassion I now have towards her. She can't help how she is. She had no choice in the matter. She struggles, but she fights for what she believes in, and she doesn't let her affliction stop her or discourage her. She doesn't give up, and that is what I admire about her. She doesn't just want acceptance, she needs acceptance, and even if no one else is willing to give her acceptance, I am, because I believe in her."

"Well, that does it then," said his father firmly. "You are grounded for a month for skipping school, lying, both to your school and to us, associating with this 'creature' and indecently exposing yourself to others. During this period, you will not watch any TV or movies, you will leave home only to go to school, you will not go to see any friends, or have any friends come over, and you will be in bed every night by nine o'clock. You know, Mark, it makes me sick that, at your age, we still have to punish you like this."

Mark said no more. He didn't care to say another word to his parents, and he wasn't in the mood to argue. There was no more point in arguing. All he wanted was to lie quietly in the hospital, waiting for his leg and chest to get better. When Mark's parents saw that their son wasn't going to say another word, they departed from his bedside, and left the hospital. Mark, relieved that his mother and father had gone, drifted back off to sleep.

18 A New Way of Life for Mark

Mark never saw Betsy in the hospital, but he did receive a card from her. It was a folded piece of cardboard, with writing, in rainbow-colored letters, that said, "I hope you get better soon. Miss you." Betsy.

On the other half of the inside of the card was a colored pencil drawing of a pretty stream, flowing over rocks, with reeds and bushes on the side.

"Oh Betsy," Mark whispered to himself. "This is wonderful. Thank you so much."

He put the card on his bedside table, so that he could see it, always.

A little while later, the nurse came to Mark's bedside. "How are you today, dear?" she asked.

Mark smiled. "Today? I am much better, thank you."

Mark was now, truly at peace. He wished he could stay in the hospital forever. He dreaded the day he would be better enough to go home, and he would see his parents again.

But then, if he never left the hospital, he would never see Betsy again either. Either way, Mark never wanted to go home, ever again.

Eventually, the day came when Mark was better enough to go home. The nurse called Mark's parents, who came to the hospital to bring him home. They hadn't stayed at the hospital for one minute, since the argument at the beginning of Mark's stay.

"Well, you're better now!" Mark's mother cried out. "I hope this teaches you never to misbehave again."

Mark rose to his feet, and stepped out of the hospital with his mom and dad. Now, it was time for Mark's grounding period to begin.

But, at that moment, Mark snapped. He was a different person; he could feel it inside. He was not going to get grounded. He wasn't going to let that happen. He was eighteen now, a young man. Mark decided, right then, that he was going to move out.

But how was he going to move out? His parents were so stern and rigid that there was no way they were going to let that happen. They would keep him shut under their roof for as long as it took them to 'correct' their son and make him a 'proper person.' Until then, even if it took Mark until he was an old man, his parents were not going to let him go.

Mark would run away from home. It was the only way. Late one night, he would pack up his belongings, call Sunny Palms, and move in, with Betsy; the girl who liked and understood him, whom he could look up to, who would save Mark from this tyrant man and woman, who had forced him to live under their roof his whole life.

But then, there was the financial issue too. If he was to move out, he was going to have to get a job. The only jobs he'd ever had, apart from his tutoring, had been his summer jobs. Then, he was right back in school every year.

He would manage, though. He had to, even if he had to find his own way in the dark, even if he had to work his fingers to the bone, even if he wasn't sure he would ever feel comfortable being undressed at Sunny Palms. He would do all of that for the sake of Betsy. Betsy was worth all of that. Betsy lived life tough. If Mark put his mind to it, he knew he could do the same.

The first thing Mark did when he arrived at home was to call Fresh Cafe. “Hello? Are you hiring?” Mark asked.

“Hello Mark,” came a man's voice on the other end. “Is that you? We've seen you quite a lot around the shop. Yes, we do have some positions available. When do you want to start?”

“As soon as possible. I have a resume from various summer

jobs. What more would you like to see?"

"For a job at our shop? Just fill out an application form. You can pick them up any time from the desk at Fresh Cafe."

"Great. I'll fill one out when I come by tomorrow before school."

Mark may have been grounded and far behind in his schoolwork, but that did not stop him from coming to Fresh Cafe the following morning to pick up an application form. He filled in everything he could think of to give himself the most opportunities for employment, while he caught up on his schoolwork.

When he completed the form, he submitted it to the hiring manager, Bill Smith, who called him for a brief interview, and announced he was hired.

The first thing Mark did when he had his job at the cafe was pack up all his belongings, (books, tent, poles, wallet, toiletries) at midnight, after his parents had gone to bed. He left the house, and headed to Sunny Palms.

Mark did not care that he was showing up, unannounced. In fact, the reaction of Sunny Palms' manager didn't even cross his mind. It never occurred to Mark that they wouldn't accept him as a member, or even a visitor, if he rudely barged his way in like this. All Mark cared about was getting away from his parents, once and for all.

Because it was the middle of the night, and no one was going to come to let him in this time of night, Mark stopped a couple hundred feet short of the gate, unpacked his tent, and set it up on the shoulder of the road. He spread out his sleeping bag on the tent floor, curled up, and slept.

Mark awoke the next morning to the sounds of birds chirping in the trees. He checked his watch, and saw that it was nine o'clock in the morning. School was starting now, but he no longer cared about school, as much as he cared about getting away from home. He disassembled his tent, stuffed it back in his pack, and headed to the gate.

Mark didn't know what to do. There was no one in sight, and here he was, unexpected, not knowing how to proceed.

Mark didn't have to wait long, however, for after a few minutes, Susan (fully clothed) showed up at the other side of the gate.

"Mark!" she cried in astonishment. "I remember you from a couple of weeks ago. What brings you back here?"

Mark's face turned white, and he began to stutter.

"Susan!" he cried. "I am so sorry to barge in like this. But, my parents, they said such awful, terrible, things about Betsy that I can't bear to stay under their roof anymore. Please let me in. I must see Betsy, and this is the only place I'll be happy."

Susan wasn't angry with Mark, but she was definitely concerned. "Mark," she explained, in sympathetic tones, "Sunny Palms is not a fortress to shut out problems. It's a place where people come to relax, in the freedom of being without clothing. We require all our visitors to contact the office beforehand and call just as they're arriving. Otherwise, we don't let people in."

Mark shook his head. "I can't go back," he said. "I would rather be in hell than in my parents' house. I am not running away into a fortress to shut out my problems. I am moving out, becoming independent. I'm of the age where I can make my own decisions, can't I?"

"Do you have a good job?" Susan asked. "If you're moving out, you need to pay your way through life."

"I work at a coffee shop, Fresh Cafe," explained Mark. "It's quite a classy place really. The workers there get paid really well."

But, with this utterance, Mark was losing confidence. Even he wasn't sure if he was up for this. Would a job at the coffee shop be enough to pay his way through life? He didn't know. As a matter of fact, he greatly doubted it. Then, Mark thought about Betsy. She lived here. How was she paying her bills to keep herself in residence?

"Hey, what does Betsy do?" Mark asked. "She doesn't have a job. How does she live here?"

"She has a friend, Catherine, who has a good job, and pays for both her own, and Betsy's expenses. Betsy's parents are also helping her."

"If you won't let me in, can you at least bring Betsy up here so that I can speak to her?"

"Well," replied Susan, "seeing as we're right by the side of the road, I won't be able to bring Betsy up here, but I can let you in to the outer limit of the resort, so that you can have a quick talk with her."

Susan opened the gate, and Mark stepped inside, still guilty about being an intruder, but excited that he could see Betsy for just a little while.

Once Mark was inside, Betsy caught sight of him, and came running up to him.

"Mark!" she called. "I'm so glad to see you. Are you better? How is your leg?"

"It still twinges a little," Mark explained, "but it's much better. It will be fine. Thank you for the card, by the way. You did a beautiful job. It really helped me feel better in the hospital."

"You're very welcome," Betsy smiled, "it was the least I could do."

"Betsy," Mark continued. "I am so sorry. My parents came when I was in the hospital and demanded to know where I had gone when they thought I was at school. They pressured me so hard that I ended up telling them about coming here and about you. I feel terrible, Betsy, like I have betrayed you. I know it was wrong, and I should have kept quiet."

"Mark," Betsy soothed. "It's okay. We're not perfect. I'm sure you did the most you could to not tell them about me."

"Thank you so much," Mark breathed in relief. "That makes me feel so much better, but I have chosen to leave home for good. I like it here, Betsy. I like being around you. I feel so much at ease and happy when I'm around you. I want to stay here forever."

Betsy smiled and nodded in understanding. "And you will," Betsy replied. "I will find a way, Mark. Don't worry."

"I got a job at Fresh Cafe," Mark explained, "but I'm not sure it's going to be enough to keep me in residence here, and I'm not sure what you will be able to do."

"I'll find some way I can get work," Betsy soothed.

"But how?"

Betsy spent the next couple of minutes thinking. While she was thinking, she remembered how Mark had appreciated the card she had made for him while he was in the hospital. "I was top of the class in most of my subjects at school," Betsy explained. "I can draw really well. Any homework I did in high school, I submitted in an envelope. For my job, I could make drawings, send them to an outlet near here, and they can sell them under my name. You and I can share the money I make."

"Betsy," Mark replied. "That's a great idea, but where will you send them?"

Betsy's smile grew. "You inspired me with the idea. Could I send them to you?"

"I can do that," Mark replied, but then he puzzled about how. There wasn't any shop handy for Mark to sell the drawings from. "But where will I work?"

"You could start out simple," Betsy suggested. "It is a new idea, and I'm not sure how well it will play out. You can start by setting up a table."

"Thank you for the advice Betsy. I have a feeling it will work out well. It's a great idea."

Then, Mark looked again at his watch.

"I'd better be heading off to school," said Mark. "I'll come back here and see you after."

"Have a good day Mark," Betsy smiled. "See you later."

Mark left for school in a daze.

At school, that day, Mark had a hard time paying attention to his teachers, and his mind was swimming with the thoughts of Betsy becoming an artist. Mark was elated. Betsy was becoming a real person at last. Even though she wouldn't be selling her drawings in person, she would be doing something useful and helpful for society.

Mark's friends felt as if there was something amiss that day. For once, Mark wasn't paying attention to them. When lunchtime came, Mark joined them in the cafeteria but he sat at the table, munching on his ham and pineapple pizza, off in his own world.

"Hey Mark!" his friend Peter finally asked. "You're such a space cadet today. What's itching you?"

"Betsy and I will be selling art," Mark smiled humbly.

"Betsy? Betsy who? You mean Betsy Parker the naked girl?" and Peter, along with the rest of Mark's friends, laughed mockingly.

"Cut it out, all of you!" Mark yelled. "I have become her friend, and I am not ashamed of who she is. She's just a little different, that's all, but she's wonderful on the inside. In her heart and spirit, she's just like you and me."

"Hey, what's got into you?" Mark's friend, Tony, jeered. "You've gone all loopy in the head. This is not like you Mark."

Mark stood up and yelled at the entire group at his table.

"Stop it!" he yelled. "Just stop this right now! You're supposed to be my friends! Friends respect each other! They stick up for each other! And they respect each other's friends too!"

There was ten seconds of silence at the table. Then, Sebastian made a mocking, snickering laugh, which was joined by a similar laugh from Tony, which was joined by Peter, and soon, the whole table was laughing, jeering, and pointing at Mark.

Mark picked up his tray and walked away. "Goodbye all of you!" he called out. "I'm eating somewhere else. You're not my friends anymore."

***

Susan let Mark back into Sunny Palms when school was out. He was still a little fazed at having lost his whole troop of friends at lunch hour, but he decided that, if he wanted to continue returning to see Betsy, he would need a membership.

"Hey Susan," Mark smiled when he saw her at the end of the school day. "I feel so happy here, everyone is so friendly, and this place is so wonderful. I would like to become a member."

"Why sure," Susan replied. "We are happy to accommodate you. Your first year as a member will be probationary. This is to ensure that all our members come for the right reason, and behave appropriately."

"I will always be on my best behavior," Mark smiled, "especially around Betsy."

Susan handed Mark a membership form, and Mark wrote down his name, address, and the rest of his personal information. He read the disclaimer which pointed out all applicable naturist etiquette, and signed his name at the bottom.

By the time Mark saw Betsy for the first time after school, that day, Mark was smiling and was eager to see her. Much to Mark's astonishment, he found that he could get out of his clothes quickly and easily this time around. It removed a barrier between himself and Betsy that Mark longed to be rid of, and he found that he could talk to her more easily, now that he was at one with her, at her level.

"Hey, how did school go?" Betsy asked him.

Mark was intrigued that she was focussed on how his day had been, and was taking no apparent notice to his state of undress.

"Oh, same old same old," Mark sighed. "It was a typical day, nothing more. I'm a member now, by the way. I filled out a form and now I have a probationary membership."

"Mark, that's wonderful!" Betsy cried. "Good for you for taking that step, and for being that accepting of me, and everyone else here."

***

Meanwhile, back at Mark's house, his parents were suspicious. They hadn't seen anything of Mark in the morning, and now that the school day was over, they still saw no sign of him.

"Where's our son?" barked Mr. Turner.

"That's what I'm wondering!" cried Mrs. Turner. "Why hasn't Mark come home? As soon as we find him, he's going to be in so much trouble, he'll wish he'd never been born."

"You don't think ... " pondered Mark's father, "I sure hope it couldn't be, but you don't think he's run off to Sunny Palms, do you?"

"Oh dear," shuddered his mother, "I've been wondering that in the back of my mind, but it's such a horrid thought I haven't really allowed myself to think about that."

"Well, I guess that's that," muttered his father. "I've been hoping we'd never have to do this, but if it's the only way to find Mark, I suppose we'll have to. We'll call the resort."

Mr. and Mrs. Turner thumbed through the phonebook until

they came to Sunny Palms. Then, Mark's father picked up the phone, and dialled.

"Sunny Palms," came Susan's voice on the other end, "how may I help you?"

"Did someone check in called Mark Turner?" asked Mark's dad. "He's our son, and we want to know if you've let him in."

"I'm sorry," replied Susan, "but for reasons of confidentiality, we do not disclose our members, or others who enter our premises, to outsiders."

"WHAT?!!" barked Mark's father.

"Anything more you need?" Susan asked.

"But what but wh eh ah DAAAAAA!" spluttered Mr. Turner, and slammed the phone down.

"What is it honey?" asked his wife. "What did they say?"

"They won't tell us!" he cried.

"Oh!" gasped Mrs. Turner.

"Well!" cried Mr. Turner, "I guess that leaves us with no alternative. I never thought, in all my life, that I'd be doing this, and I really don't want to have to, but Mark has left us with no choice."

"And what's that dear?"

"Drive to Sunny Palms and get our son out!"

"Brian!" protested Mark's mother. "No! We can't! We won't! We mustn't! We're not going anywhere near that ghastly place! There has to be another way!"

"Do you want to stop our son from mingling with these perverts or not?!" yelled Mr. Turner.

"Of course I do, but, oh Brian! For mercy's sake, we can't go in there!"

"We don't have to go in!" he yelled. "We just have to go to the gate! Now come on!"

Slowly, and shaking, as though they were walking on a bed of nails, Mark's parents made their way to their car. Mark's father started the car, and they drove away.

***

Meanwhile, back at the resort, Betsy and Mark were talking about how they would market Betsy's art.

"We'll set up a website to advertise your work," Mark beamed, "and the site will be called 'The World in the eyes of Betsy Parker' and it will have the URL www.theworldintheeyesofbetsy.com. People will come from far and wide to buy your drawings. I just know it."

"Aw shucks," smiled Betsy, with a laugh in her eyes and face. "I don't know if I'll be that popular, but if I can sell at least some drawings, I'll be over the moon."

"I can buy you your art supplies," Mark promised her, "then you can make your art here. I will take your drawings to my table and sell them as having been made by you. This is going to work, Betsy. I can just feel it."

Right then, a hollering noise echoed over Betsy, Mark's and the other nudists' shoulders.

"What was that?" Betsy cried.

"I don't know," stuttered Mark. "It sounded like a dying wolf."

The noise sounded again.

"MMMAAAAAAAAAARRRKKK!!!" it went.

"It's someone yelling 'Mark!'" Mark cried. "Betsy, it's calling me!"

The noise sounded a third time, and, this time, Betsy and Mark noticed that it was coming from the gate.

"Oh for heaven's sake!" Mark stammered. "It's my parents. Never mind them, Betsy. I'm not going anywhere near there. They can go away on their own."

"MMMMMAAAAAAAAAAAAAAAAAAAARRRRRRRRR RKKKKK!!!!!" shouted the voices of Mark's father and mother together from just outside the gate.

"Susan will take care of them. Don't worry Betsy. I'm eighteen and moved out. All they're doing is making idiots of themselves."

"Mark, they're your parents!" cried Betsy.

"So?" he responded in a purely indifferent voice.

"Maybe you should go over and reason with them. You might be able to work something out."

"Yeah ... sure," Mark laughed, "might as well reason with a doorknob while I'm at it."

After the next bellowing of "Mark" echoed from the gate and all the way across the grounds, Susan approached Mark.

"Your parents are calling you," she explained. "I think you had better go over, and see what it's about. They're disturbing the entire resort with their wailing."

Mark still didn't want to go. He turned to watch Susan, who walked over, in the direction towards the gate.

"I'll go," said Betsy. "Even if you won't go, Mark, I will."

"Oh Betsy!" cried Mark. "Not you. That will be the worst of it."

Nonetheless, Betsy walked, with Susan, towards the gate.

Mark sighed. This was it. If he was going to stay Betsy's friend, and keep a strong reputation with Susan, he'd have to go to the gate to face his parents. Slowly, and reluctantly, Mark hobbled his way over to the gate too.

When the trio arrived at the entrance of Sunny Palms, there were Mark's parents as red faced, and furious as a pair of TNT bombs blowing up.

"MARK EDWARD TURNER!!! YOU GET DRESSED THIS INSTANT!!!" hollered Mark's father, when he saw his son.

"What's with all the catterwalling?!" cried Susan. "You're disturbing the peace of our campers, both of you!"

Neither of Mark's parents acted as though they had heard Susan.

"AND YOU MARK!!!" Mark's father yelled so furiously, that Mark wouldn't have been surprised if his head had exploded. "GET AWAY FROM THAT CREATURE YOU CALL BETSY!!!!!"

"You are getting away from this gate even if I have to drive you away myself!" Susan yelled. "You're making a mighty embarrassment of yourselves, the two of you!"

By now, several other campers, either clothed, or wrapped in towels, were arriving behind the gate, and they all began yelling at Mark's parents that this was a private resort and that they had to leave. Meanwhile, Mark's parents continued hollering that their son was coming home.

In a matter of seconds, the din grew to being so bombastic that no one could be heard anymore.

"NO!!!" Mark yelled, and he had an adrenalyn rush so powerful, that his voice carried above his parents and the campers. The entire racket stopped in silence.

"I AM ***NOT*** COMING HOME WITH YOU!!!" Mark yelled, when all was quiet. "MY HOME IS HERE! WITH BETSY!"

Mark was shaking and sniffling and badly beaten up inside, but he was determined to get his message out.

"I am a man!" Mark cried. "I am not a boy anymore. I am eighteen and that makes me legally an adult. I have a job, I can pay my own bills and I have moved out!"

"Young man!" yelled his father. "You have not moved out! You are coming home, with us, now, and if you think you are living with these sickos, which includes Betsy, you are mistaken. Not until you have learned decency and respect for your parents will you be allowed to leave our roof."

"I don't care!" Mark yelled. "I am not coming to live under your prison of a house even if you have to kill me! Betsy is not an animal, she is not a pervert, she is not an exhibitionist, and neither are any of my friends who live here or visit here! ... And ... Neither am I. And I am not your pet to take home with you!"

Mark's father made a grab at his son, so suddenly that Mark didn't even have a chance to avoid it, in an attempt to force him over the gate to carry him into the car. "Now you nasty, filthy son of a ..."

And Mark, with his full adrenalyn rush still reeling, punched his father in the stomach with a giant blow, and the large crowd that had gathered gasped.

Mrs. Turner looked on in horror, as she watched her husband collapse onto the ground, gasping, winded, in pain, huffing and puffing to regain his air.

Mark returned to his senses. "I'm sorry," he sobbed, tears streaming down his cheeks. "I didn't mean to do that. Are you okay dad?"

"Bye bye Mark," his mother sobbed. "Just goodbye. For good. We are no longer your parents. We never knew you, and you are a filthy disgrace, a disease to our family tree."

Mark's father stood back on his feet and made one more breath for air. "It's over," Mr. Turner muttered. "Go live with that creature, Betsy. See if we care. We don't have two sons, Mark. We have one son, and his name is Roger. We are disowning you. You are dead to both of us. We'll build a big bonfire in our back yard when we get home and we'll burn every picture of you, everything that reminds us of you, and everything that belongs to you. We will have nothing more to do with you."

Mark's father turned back to his wife. "Come on Margaret. Let's get out of here. I feel filthy and disgraced that we ever came to this place."

And Brian and Margaret Turner departed from the gate of Sunny Palms, while the campers dispersed to continue their afternoon in the sun.

19 The Art Sale

Mark should have been proud that he had driven his parents away. Since their arrival at the gate where they started bull roaring for him, the only thing Mark had wanted was for them to get lost. He had wanted that so much he'd been willing to do anything to get that, and that was precisely what Mark had done.

But Mark felt guilty. He was not a violent person, but he had hit his own father ... in the presence of *Betsy!*

What was Betsy going to think of him now? Was she going to think of Mark as some abusive, violent, dangerous assailant, and leave him? Had their plans to become artists shattered? If Betsy didn't want to work with Mark anymore, because of this, was Mark going to crumble financially because he might not be able to make an adequate living to reside at Sunny Palms on his own?

"Betsy," Mark stuttered, as the two of them walked away from the gate, "I ..."

He looked at Betsy's face. She was upset, but was she upset with him? Mark hoped, oh please, not.

"Mark," Betsy sighed. "I'm sorry it had to come to that."

"Please!" Mark cried. "Please don't be mad at me! I've never hit anyone in my life, and I wouldn't hit you if someone held a gun to my head."

"I know," Betsy replied, in a soothing voice. "You're not that kind of person Mark. I actually think you were very brave."

"You do? I mean, I wasn't trying to be brave, Betsy. I didn't want to put on a show or anything. I just wanted my parents to go away. In the end, after everything they were doing to me and after everything they were saying about you, my fist just shot out from me, like I didn't even have control over it."

"Thank you for defending me," Betsy smiled. "Don't feel bad Mark. It's unfortunate it had to come to this, but I think, in the end, it was the only way."

"Yeah," Mark nodded. "I just feel bad that you had to see that."

"There's no need to feel bad," explained Betsy, in soft comforting tones. "They were kidnapping you, Mark. You had announced that you'd moved out of their home to live here, and they had no right to disrespect that. You have every moral and legal right to live wherever you choose."

"Thank you Betsy," Mark smiled. "It's so comforting to have someone who understands."

Betsy smiled at Mark in return.

"And Betsy," Mark continued, "all those things my parents said about you, you can forget about that. I know that is not what you're like."

"I know," Betsy beamed. "Thank you for understanding and accepting me, Mark. It's what I have wanted my whole life. Honestly, I never dreamed I would make it this far, but" Betsy breathed a sigh of love and happiness, "here I am," and she spread her arms open wide to embrace all the beauty around her.

"So," Mark smiled. "I think it's time we got started on some artwork, don't you?"

"Absolutely!" cried Betsy in delight. "Just let me take a little walk around the grounds, find something to inspire me."

"We'll walk together," Mark smiled, "I'm still getting used to this place and my skin could use some sun and fresh air."

Mark and Betsy walked along the lawn, feeling the grass on their feet, looking at the trees, and onto the lake.

"Oh look," smiled Betsy, peering out onto the water.

There, sitting on the lake, was a duck. It was mottled brown, had miniature streaks of white among its wings, and had a blue-green beak.

“That's such a pretty duck,” Betsy smiled. “I think I'll draw that.”

Betsy, who had been carrying her pencils and sketchbook with her since they had begun their walk, started her work on drawing the duck as it paddled along on the water. Not only did she draw the duck itself, but she also drew the water around it and the ripples it made along the water.

When she had finished, she showed her drawing to Mark.

“Wow!” Mark cried in admiration of Betsy. “You are amazing. That duck just looks like it's going to fly up and out of the page any instant.”

“I'll keep making more drawings throughout the week while you're in school,” Betsy suggested. “Then, over the weekend, when you have more time, you can set up your table and sell what I have made.”

“That sounds like a great plan,” Mark commented. “Where should I set my table up?” he asked himself. “I know. How about down the road, at the turn off just up ahead? It's only a few hundred feet away, and the people who buy your drawings might feel drawn to come up to Sunny Palms and meet you, the real artist.”

“Thanks Mark,” replied Betsy, “but I don't want that much attention. I just want to get my work out.”

“I understand,” Mark replied, “but I think, whilst you're just getting started, the corner down the road will attract just the right amount of attention; enough that you can say you're selling, but not enough so that there are people in your face all the time. Then, when you get to be more pronounced, I can move my sales place somewhere more far away. There's a vacant lot next to the supermarket that I think would be good.”

"That's a good plan, Mark," Betsy smiled. "I will keep drawing."

And Betsy did. After drawing the duck on the lake, she drew the lake itself. Then, she drew a panorama of the trees that lined the sky. She drew a gorgeous sunset one evening. It was red, pink, purple, yellow, gold, mauve, magenta, and many other colors, and Betsy caught every single color and texture perfectly.

At the end of the week, Mark bought a table. It was a round, wooden table, easy to fold up and carry around.

He presented the table to Betsy, who reacted with joy at how elegant it was. "Wow!" she cried. "Great choice. That will be perfect for my art."

When Friday arrived, Betsy gave Mark the drawings she had made, each one inscribed with her signature, so that her buyers could know it was really her. Mark put them in his bag, carried the table out of Sunny Palms and set it up just down the road. Mark sat, by the table, awaiting the first customers. Would anyone come? Surely someone would. If Mark had walked by an art table on a whim, and seen drawings of this quality, he wouldn't have been able to resist buying them for anything.

After a twenty-minute wait, a middle-aged man on the roadside passed by and caught sight of the table and the artwork.

"Oh my!" he cried when he saw what Mark had to sell. "These are wonderful. Did you make these all by yourself?"

"Actually, they're not mine at all," Mark explained. "I didn't raise a finger, or a colored pencil, to create any of these. I am the salesman only. If you want to know the artist, all you need to do is read the signature."

As the man gazed at what the signature on the drawings read, Mark awaited, in suspense, for his response. Was he going to react in shock and horror when he saw that they had been made by Betsy?

Would the mere fact that it was her that had made him, drive this man away?

"Betsy Parker," he murmured as he read the signature. "Hey, I know who that is."

The man broke out in a smile that split his face. "Wow!" he cried. "Betsy is getting into art? These drawings are incredible. She is so talented."

"She is," Mark smiled. "I am proud of her."

"And who are you?" the man continued. "Her sales partner? Her friend?"

"You could say I'm her friend," Mark explained, "but my feelings towards her are growing deeper and stronger over time. Betsy has such a smile, such a character, and she really makes me feel like a child once again. She's just, so much her own person."

"Yeah, she would be," the man smiled. "Name is Douglas, by the way. Douglas Smith. I will be happy to buy one of these. I think I'll buy this duck right here."

Douglas picked his wallet out of his pocket, and handed Mark twenty-five dollars. Mark took the money and handed him Betsy's drawing of the duck.

"This will be such a treasure," Douglas smiled. "I will go right home, and put this on my mantelpiece. Thank you. I will treasure it forever."

"Thank you for your interest," Mark smiled, as Douglas stepped away from the table. "I am so thankful you appreciate Betsy's artwork."

After another eight-minute wait, a mother with two children, an older girl and a younger boy, showed up. The mother noticed the signature.

"Betsy made these?" the mother cried, amazed.

"She sure did," Mark smiled, "and I'm selling them to anyone who wants to buy them."

"Michelle, Craig," she said to her children, "which one do you like the most?"

"I like the butterfly one," the girl, whom the mother had addressed as Michelle, smiled.

"The sunset one is really cool," the boy, Craig, grinned.

"You know," the mother smiled to Mark. "I think we'll buy both."

"Sure thing," Mark grinned. He took the fifty the mother handed them, and gave her both drawings.

From then on, Mark's table was wild with customers. There were ladies, gentlemen, boys and girls coming from everywhere to buy a drawing. Eventually, it got to a point where there was a line-up, and, about two hours after Mark had set up his table, he sold out.

Mark was ecstatic. He folded the table back up, spread his arms wide and cheered.

"Oh Betsy!" he cried, still at his sales site, even though Betsy wasn't there to hear him. "We did it! You're a success Betsy! The whole town loves you!"

Mark was so cheerful and excited that he ran back to Sunny Palms, even though he was carrying the heavy, wooden table. When he got to the gate, Susan let him back in. He put the table down in the entrance, and ran across the grounds to meet Betsy.

"Mark!" she cried. "You're back early. By the way you're acting, it must have gone well."

"Betsy!" he cried. "It's Christmas! It went better than well! Everything went, Betsy. I sold everything!"

Betsy's smile broke into a laugh. "Everything Mark? You sold everything? On only our first day? Mark, that's ... fantastic!"

"What do you want to do now, Betsy? Anything you want. You deserve it."

"Let's go for a walk in the woods," Betsy replied. "It's so peaceful there, and you deserve some rest, peace and quiet after all you've done."

And so, Mark and Betsy took a walk in the woods. It was peaceful for both of them. The shaded air was cool and the ground was soft.

"Whatever I make from my art, we will donate half the proceedings to charity," Betsy beamed.

Mark smiled back at her. "Of course we will," he grinned. "I'm proud of how generous you are."

When Mark and Betsy stepped out of Sunny Palms' forest, back into the open lawn once again, Catherine was waiting for Betsy, and smiling.

"Betsy," Catherine grinned, her blue eyes shining in the late-afternoon sun. "I am so proud of you, selling so much of your work on your first day. Please come with me. Someone has arrived, who would like to meet you."

Betsy and Mark followed Catherine to the office, where a man was waiting, whom Mark recognized right away.

"Douglas!" Mark cried out. "You're here! How do you like this place?"

"I just came to give my congratulations to the real artist," Douglas smiled.

Betsy stepped forward. "I am Betsy," she explained. "I created that art work. Do you like it?"

"Like it?" he beamed, in a smile of pure delight and admiration. "Betsy Parker, I love it. My name is Douglas, by the way. I was one of Mark's customers."

"The first one," Mark explained. "He bought your duck."

"And it was an awesome duck," Douglas nodded. "Betsy, you captured everything in that picture. You could become the next

Picasso, really."

"Thank you," she smiled, "no one has ever given me this much appreciation for something I did, ever. I'm not even sure what to make of it."

"Ah," Douglas smiled at Betsy, looking her in the eyes, "You did a wonderful job, and that is all that matters. Keep up the good work."

"So how long are you down here for?" asked Mark.

"Just until this evening," Douglas replied. "I've never been to a place like this before, and I thought I'd start out with a brief visit, just to try it out, and meet the artist in person."

"Well thank you for buying my picture. I'm glad you like it," replied Betsy, with a humble smile.

"Thank you for making it, Betsy," Douglas continued. "I'll be going back to my tent now. Nice talking to you."

And the man departed.

"Such a nice man," Mark beamed, "well all the people at the sale were nice. Things are getting better for you, Betsy. I can feel it."

"I can feel it to," Betsy replied. "Come on Mark, after this successful day, I think I'm about ready to set up my website."

"You bet, Betsy," Mark grinned. "I agree wholeheartedly."

20 Mark's Proposal

Douglas was the only person from the sale that came to Sunny Palms that day. Betsy felt it was just as well. She, and the other campers, didn't want to be bothered by a swarm of new people entering the grounds all in one day. Mark had studied computer science in school. He had learned basic programming and how to set up a website. His first step was to choose a background for the site.

"I think I'd like a lush meadow background, with a lake and a waterfall," smiled Betsy.

Mark skimmed through the kinds of site designs available, and found just the one Betsy requested. Mark installed it on the screen, created the URL www.theworldintheeyesofbetsy.com and uploaded the photographs of the many works of art Betsy had created. He and Betsy negotiated pricing for every work, and Mark added the price to the website.

When the website was complete, Betsy and Mark were overjoyed.

"What do you think?" Mark asked. "Do you like it?"

"It's amazing!" Betsy cried. "Thank you so much."

"When you create a new work, just click on this pencil icon to upload it," Mark explained, "and this dollar-sign to add a price."

Then, Mark's expression turned clouded.

"What's wrong?" Betsy asked him.

"Betsy," he sighed. "I'm going to be graduating from high school at the end of this year, and I don't want you to miss it. It's not going to be a happy graduation if you're not there. You had to miss your own graduation. I don't want you to have to miss mine."

"Mark," Betsy sighed, "don't worry about me. You'll have a good time, and I'm sure there will be loads of pictures. We can look at them together when you come home, and we'll think happy thoughts then."

"But it won't be the same," Mark continued. "I won't have a date, Betsy. The only person I would ever ask on a date for my grad is you, but grad's at school, and you're here, and I would never be accepted with you, you and I walking down the red carpet together. Betsy, there is no one else I would go with. No one."

Betsy looked Mark in the eyes. A little endearing laugh crossed her face. "Mark," Betsy smiled, "you love me, don't you?"

Mark looked back at her and nodded. "I love you, Betsy; with all my heart, with all the world, with everything."

"I've always known that," Betsy grinned.

"So have I," Mark admitted.

Betsy sighed and looked thoughtfully at Mark. "Maybe the day after your grad, we could celebrate your finishing high school right here, on our own."

"I will be satisfied with that," Mark replied, although he wasn't certain he really would be. "It won't be the same as having you with me for the real thing, but as long as I can celebrate with you in some form, I will be happy."

The next weekend, Mark sold more of Betsy's art. These pictures at Mark's sales table included colored pencil drawings, pastel drawings, and watercolor paintings. Betsy had made more than what she had previously made, so the sale went on for longer. Still, her pictures were so popular that, once again, there was a line-up.

An hour or so into the sale, Mark was startled by a couple who caught his eyes in a very strange way. They looked like people he knew from somewhere, but he couldn't think where, and he couldn't take his eyes off their faces. In fact, the more he looked, the more resemblance he saw to Betsy. In between them was a teenage girl, who looked similar to Betsy too.

On the spur of the moment, Mark took note of what he was doing. “Sorry,” he said, “I shouldn't have done that. It's rude to stare. I just, feel like I know you.”

“You do?” asked the woman of the pair. “I'm not sure we know you. My name is Megan Parker. We flew down for our daughter's art sale.”

Mark's mouth dropped wide open. “You're Betsy's parents?” he cried. “Wow! It's a real pleasure to meet you. Anything you want, I'll let you have it for half-price.”

“There's no need,” explained the father. “As long as it's our daughter's, we'll gladly take anything for full price. My name's Carl, by the way.”

For the moment, Mark forgot that he was supposed to be selling and proceeded to introduce himself to Betsy's parents. “I'm Mark,” he explained, “Mark Turner. I'm Betsy's friend, and sales partner.”

“Well, congratulations Mark!” Megan cried in delight. “I'm so delighted that Betsy has made a friend close enough to her to sell for her. It's a shame she can't come out here and sell her work herself.”

“Mom!” the girl in between them cried. “Please don't be an embarrassment. I would be mortified if Betsy came out here.”

“That must be Laura,” Mark commented.

“She is,” smiled Megan.

Laura blushed.

“Come on, sweetheart. This is your sister's art. Aren't you proud of her?”

“It's nice,” Laura said casually.

“How long are you down for?” Mark asked.

“Us? Oh Mark, we've moved. We're here to stay,” Carl explained. “When we heard our daughter was an artist, we were so elated that we wanted to stay by her side, unceasingly, and support her."

"Here to stay?" Mark asked, intrigued. "Will you be coming to Sunny Palms? I'm sure Betsy is missing you."

"NO!!!" Laura hollered.

Megan chuckled. "Not with Laura anyway. We'll definitely be coming down in the near future. I think Laura's grown up enough she can look after herself for a while. Betsy doesn't know we've come down here. I think we'll arrange a visit with the manager, then pop in and surprise Betsy. Please don't say anything to her until then, Mark. I'd really prefer it to be a surprise."

"Okay," Mark said. "My lips are sealed. Anyway, what would you like to buy?"

"I think I'll buy this pretty little robin right here," Carl smiled.

"I'll take the flowerbed," beamed Megan. Then, she turned to her younger daughter. "Anything for you, Laura?"

Laura sighed. She looked around at the drawings.

"The thorn bush," Laura muttered at last. "I'll take the thorn bush."

It was a pretty drawing, just like all of Betsy's, but not one of her more attractive ones. Betsy had drawn it because *she* thought it looked beautiful. It was a plant in the garden, just outside Betsy's cabin, surrounded by many other beautiful, colorful, non-thorny plants. Still, Betsy had drawn every plant in that garden as individual pictures, as well as one picture of the garden as a whole. Although Betsy was now a successful artist, she was still an excluded girl in the human race, and she did not want to exclude anything in nature. Therefore, she had drawn the thorn bush, as an equal plant to all the others.

"Laura," her mother assured her, "there are so many other wonderful pictures here; why take the thorn bush?"

"Because it's the one I want," Laura insisted.

"All right, Laura," Mark smiled, and handed Laura the thorn bush.

The Parkers paid, smiled at Mark one last time, and moved on until they were out of sight.

Mark and Betsy's sales pitch was a success, but it was not perfect. Mark had one customer come forward with a sinister, accusatory expression.

"This is your art, isn't it?" he grumbled.

"No," Mark explained, "this is Betsy's art, and I am proud of her for making it."

"No!" the man insisted, "It's your art. You made all this, Mark. You're only selling it under Betsy's name to draw attention to her."

"What the?" Mark cried, "are you calling me a fraud? For your information, if I had made work of this quality, I would be far too proud of it to sell it under anyone else's name. You're not a customer; you're a naysayer. Next!" Mark called to the people behind the man.

***

Later that day, at the resort, Mark and Betsy were relaxing in Betsy's pool. Catherine approached Betsy, "You have some visitors dear," she smiled.

Betsy looked over her shoulder.

"Mom! Dad!" she screamed, and, in a great splash, dashed out of her pool and ran up to her parents.

"There you are, my darling," Megan cried, "We are so happy to see you, and we're so proud of you too. Congratulations on becoming such a success."

"I'm only half the success. I draw; Mark sells everything."

"So I've heard," Betsy's mother beamed at both Mark and

Betsy.

"Still no Laura?" Betsy asked.

"No," Carl replied. "I'm sorry Betsy, but I don't think you're going to see anything of Laura again. She's a sweet kid, she really is, but she's shy, and very conformist. She doesn't want to risk sticking out like a sore thumb."

"Yeah, I suppose," Betsy sighed. "How is Laura doing?"

"She's doing well in school," Carl informed Betsy. "She had a boyfriend from her home high school that she really misses because of the move."

"Boyfriend? Home high school? Mom! Dad! What do you mean?"

"We've moved," explained Betsy's mother. "We have decided to come and live with you, Betsy. We love you too much to let you go. We are so inspired by your work."

"Poor Laura," Betsy cried, "you took her away from her boyfriend? Don't you think that was rather harsh?"

"Can't say it was an easy choice," Carl explained, "but it was either stay at our old home for Laura's sake, or come here for yours. I'm not saying that you're our pet, Betsy. We love Laura just as much as we love you, but the relationship was breaking up already. We knew it wasn't going to last, and Laura didn't think so either. We felt you were the one more in need of familial companionship. Laura still misses her boyfriend, Carlos, but they keep in touch as pen-pals, and the relationship has dropped to a casual friendship."

"This is so wrong!" Betsy protested. "How could you do this? There was enough distance between me and Laura already, without you taking her away from the boy she loved for my sake and making it worse."

"Betsy!" cried her father, "she didn't love him. Even Laura is getting over it now. Please try to do the same."

"Excuse me," said Betsy, "I have some drawing to do."

She departed from the pool.

When Betsy arrived at her house, she took her notepad and some colored pencils, and set herself to work on a drawing. She locked the door and drew continuously for three hours. The end result was a drawing of Mark, in a tuxedo, herself in her birthday suit, herself and Mark holding hands, walking down the red carpet at Mark's graduation. All the people on Mark's side of the walk were shocked and furious, while all the people on Betsy's side were happy, jubilant, and cheering for Mark and Betsy.

When Betsy finished this picture, she ripped its page out of her note pad, slammed the notepad shut, shut the one page containing the picture in her bedside drawer, and locked the drawer.

"I am not showing that picture to anyone!" Betsy cried. "Especially Mark. I will keep it to myself, and no one else will even know it exists."

In the months that followed, no one ever did discover the existence of that picture. But, all the same, an exciting sequence of events rolled on. Mark was a busy young man, living at the resort, going to school, doing his homework, working at Fresh Cafe, and selling Betsy's art. A countless number of people were coming to buy Betsy's art, either in person, or online. As a result of Betsy's popularity, the number of members and visitors at Sunny Palms had tripled. By this time, even the managers were having a hard time keeping track of everyone, and were considering expanding the grounds.

"Hey! Look at all the members and visitors," Mark commented. "I have never seen anything like this. Your art has also become a gateway to market nudism."

"I don't care how many people come here," Betsy explained, "I only care about expressing my work. I don't paint and draw to bring people to this place. I do it because it has become my living and it's what I like to do."

Finally, it was early June, and the day of Mark's graduation arrived.

"Today's the day," Mark smiled at Betsy. "Wish me luck."

"I do," Betsy smiled back, "with all my heart."

Mark dressed himself in the tuxedo he had rented, and showed himself to Betsy.

"You look very handsome," Betsy smiled at him, but, as Betsy said this, Mark noticed Betsy's lower lip tremble.

"You okay Bess?" he asked her.

"Just have a good grad," Betsy replied. "I'm proud of you, Mark. Have a great day."

And off Mark went.

He arrived at the high school on foot, and nestled himself in with the other twelfth grade boys. Mark's parents were nowhere to be seen, but Mark didn't care. They wanted nothing more to do with him, and, quite frankly, he didn't want anything more to do with them, either. After a few minutes, the first grad couple walked across the red carpet, and everyone, including Mark, cheered. It was Evan White and Mary Maxwell from his chemistry class, smiling and waving as they walked hand in hand.

One after another, more and more pairs walked the carpet. Some students Mark knew, others he didn't. Some were Mark's former friends that he'd left because of that incident in the cafeteria. Nonetheless, Mark cheered for them all, even the people he no longer cared about so much. On the odd occasion, there was a boy going stag, but the applause was wild and joyous all the same. There was one girl who was by herself too, but the fact that she was alone didn't seem to spoil her enthusiasm and everyone cheered. On two instances, a same-sex pair walked the carpet. One was both boys, the other both girls.

Finally, the principal called, "Mark Turner." Mark knew that this was his cue and it was time for him to walk the carpet, alone.

Mark shuffled his feet down the bleachers where the rest of the boys were standing. It was almost impossible to walk. His legs felt like they were made of sticks, and his feet felt like they were made of rubber. Mark was trembling and sweating as well.

"You okay Mark?" his former friend, Sebastian, asked him.

"Yeah ..." Mark stuttered, "fine."

He climbed off the bleachers and walked robotically towards the edge of the carpet, looking at his feet the whole time. At long last, when he arrived at the carpet, he set a toe on the edge.

Whispers echoed from all around.

"Where's he going?" echoed some whispers.

"He's nervous," he heard others whispering.

"He's not going to do it," whispered some others.

Mark began to take a few steps along the carpet, but he walked slowly and hesitantly, as though he were wading his way into icy water. As he walked, he began to shiver, and he reached out his hand to the Betsy who wasn't there.

Suddenly, a loud voice startled Mark.

"Hey Mark!" the principal called. "That's the exiting end of the carpet. You're walking the wrong way!"

Mark's head jerked to glance the full length of the carpet, and he turned to face his surroundings. The principal was right. Mark had entered the carpet on the exiting end and was walking in the wrong direction. It was then that Mark noticed that the whispers around him had changed to puzzlement and surprise, in wonder of where the heck Mark was going.

Mark's hurt turned to fury, and his eyes burned with tears. He turned and ran. He ran and ran until he was as far away as he could get himself from his graduation. He didn't even stop when he arrived back at the gate of Sunny Palms. He clambered over the gate, and, still in his tuxedo, ran across the grounds. He didn't stop until he came face to face, once more, with Betsy.

"Mark!" Betsy cried. "What happened?"

But Betsy already knew. She answered the question for him. "You couldn't stay, could you? You couldn't bear to walk that carpet without me."

"Yeah," he replied. "It just wasn't graduation without you. I wouldn't miss being with you for the world."

"Well, you're here with me now," Betsy soothed, "and that is all that matters."

"Betsy?" Mark stuttered. "I have been dying to ask you for some time. It's just that, things wouldn't be the same for us, as they are with most people who do this sort of thing, but..."

Mark paused, mustering all the courage he had so that he could form the words on his lips.

"Betsy, will you marry me?"

Betsy's smile broke into a laugh of merriment to end the world.

"Oh Mark!" she cried, "Yes, of course I will marry you!"

"Yes?!" Mark cried, "Did I hear that correctly? Did you really say 'yes'?"

"I did," Betsy smiled. "We'll be happy together, I know it."

With a tender, gentle hand, Betsy wiped the tears off of Mark's cheeks with her fingers.

"Betsy," Mark smiled, as feelings of love, comfort and warmth bubbled inside him, "thank you for accepting my proposal. It's the best thing I have heard today, in my entire life actually."

21 A Joyous Celebration

Mark's first task, after becoming engaged to Betsy, was to find a clergyman who was willing to perform the ceremony. He doubted it would be an easy task. He was aware of the Bible's story of Adam and Eve living naked in the Garden of Eden, but then God clothing them and expelling them from the garden after they ate the forbidden fruit. Mark knew that there would be many ministers who would adhere to God's clothing of Adam and Eve and view that as being more important than the fact that the couple had once been naked and unashamed, and therefore Betsy, as Mark's parents had tried to tell him, was a creature of the devil.

Mark had been to church. His parents had taken him and Roger every week when Mark was a little boy, but Mark was never interested in the minister, Bob Jones's, sermons. Mark had always found them dry, tedious and quite preachy. Additionally, being a "Turner approved" minister, Mark knew that Bob would rather die than perform Betsy and Mark's wedding. Mark decided to turn to Betsy to consult with her.

"Betsy?" he asked, "do you know of anyone who might be willing to marry us?"

Betsy sighed and looked thoughtful. "I wasn't born like this," she explained.

Mark looked at her, stunned. "Betsy, what are you talking about? Everybody is born naked. Don't try to tell me that you already had clothes on when you came out of the womb. Now that really would be something."

By the way Betsy looked at Mark, he knew he had hurt her, and he felt terrible about what he had just said.

"I'm sorry Betsy. That was such a thoughtless thing to say. I promise you, I will never ever make another remark like that again, but what do you mean by not being born like this?"

"I wasn't born with the kind of reaction I have to this day," she explained. "I lived my first few months as a normal baby, able to wear a diaper, clothes and be a normal baby girl. I was far too young to remember any of it. I only know because my parents told me. They had me baptized and Christened when I was a week old, when I could still wear clothes, when my parents had no clue of what was coming up for me. My minister who did that baptism and Christening came to our house once a month, every month, starting when I was four years old, so that he could encourage and support me, and he was so happy, so open to me. His name was Reverend Ben Herb. He would be willing to perform our wedding ceremony. I just know it."

Mark and Betsy looked up Reverend Ben Herb on the internet. "He lives in your former area," Mark explained, "but I'll message him and ask him if he can come down here to perform our wedding."

Mark did so, and, only a few hours later, received a reply.

Dear Mark Turner,

I am blown away. What's this I hear about Betsy Parker getting married? That charming little girl I came to visit all those years ago? Since learning about her never being able to wear clothes, I spent many sleepless nights praying for her. But here she is, an artist, with a gentleman who loves her, and is taking her as his wife. Perhaps this is a sign from God that the Garden of Eden is returning. Mark, don't you worry about a thing. I will marry you and her. I would do anything to do this. May your and her years together be long on this planet. You couldn't have made a better choice for a wife. You are blessed.

Rev. Ben Herb

PS The chocolate Santa was delicious!

"Yes!" cried Mark when he finished reading the email. "Betsy! We did it! We are getting married!"

"It's going to be wonderful," Betsy wept. "I'll be counting down the days."

Betsy's first task, after reading the minister's message, was to make wedding invitations. She designed a card, featuring a drawing of a bouquet of flowers and a pair of rings. She inscribed the following message:

We, Betsy Alicia Parker and Mark Edward Turner, will be celebrating our marriage at Sunny Palms naturist resort at 3:00 pm August 22. Reception to follow in the clubhouse.

Mark took the many copies of the invitation that Betsy had made, and sent them to Betsy's parents, to Laura, to the students who had come to visit her when she was in high school, to the Nelsons and to the Barnes's. All the guests and members of Sunny Palms were welcome to attend as well.

"I've sent your invitations out, Betsy," Mark told her. "I won't be anticipating that anyone from my family will be attending, but I'm hoping there will be a strong turnout from your family, and everyone else you know."

Mark paused, in thought, for another moment, "You know, Betsy. I know I have severed all ties with my family, but I think I'll go and see Roger. I won't ask him to come to the wedding, but I would just like him to know that I'm getting married to you."

"But Mark," Betsy gasped, in surprise. "You said, yourself, that you rejoiced at never having to see Roger again."

"I did," Mark paused, "I do, but he is still my brother, and maybe deep down inside he's inspired enough by how we feel about each other that he will at least give his blessing."

Mark knew these words were complete baloney, but he was determined, all the same, to at least try to rebuild a bond with his brother, since his parents were out of the question.

"And you have inspired me to love people unconditionally," Mark added.

Betsy smiled, "Really? That's wonderful Mark. You're right. He is your brother, and I am proud of you for choosing to see him again. I wish you luck."

"I'll need it," Mark smiled. He got dressed, walked across the grounds, and departed out the gate.

Roger lived a half-hour drive from Mark's house. Mark decided that he would walk home, get his car, and drive to Roger's house. Mark didn't count on the car being at his home anymore, as his parents had said they would burn everything that was his. They wouldn't be able to burn the car, but they could always sell it.

Alas, when he arrived at what was formerly his house, his fear was confirmed. His car was gone, and nowhere to be seen. Mark did the only thing he could think of doing, and awaited the Hele-On Bus. He walked to the end of the street, as he didn't want to be anywhere near that house anyway, and his parents wouldn't want to see him in front of their yard.

The bus arrived, and a stout-looking man was sitting behind the wheel.

When the bus stopped in front of Roger's house, Mark stepped out, and walked, with hesitation, down Roger's driveway. Then, with trembling knuckles, Mark knocked on Roger's door.

When the door opened, a snarly-faced, black-haired young man was standing on the other side. It was Roger.

"Hey you!" Roger snarled, when he saw Mark, "What brings filth like yourself to my house?"

"Betsy and I are getting married," Mark replied.

"Look you," grunted Roger in a menacing manner, and staring straight into Mark's eyes, "If you think you are asking me to that naked so-and-so's wedding, you've got another think coming."

"I'm not asking you to come to the wedding," Mark insisted, "I only want your blessing. You are my brother after all."

"You hit my dad!" Roger snapped.

"Look," Mark admitted, "even I feel bad about doing that, but-"

"And you're not my brother either," Roger hissed. "You're disowned, remember. You chose to live with that Betsy weirdo. Make up your mind who you want to live with, and stop bothering me."

By now, Mark knew it was no good. He had tried to convince his parents of the loving, peaceful, nature of Betsy, but it had failed dismally. He was not going to be able to do the same thing to Roger, no matter what Mark said or did, or how hard he tried.

"Well, bye then," said Mark. "I will stop bothering you. I didn't really want to come here in the first place, but the least I wanted was to let you know."

"I would rather be tortured to death in the Chamber of Horrors than come within a hundred-yard radius of Betsy!" Roger hollered, blowing a raspberry out of the 'B' in 'Betsy.'

Roger slammed the door, and Mark walked away.

"Well, I guess that's that," Mark sighed to himself, as the bus driver drove him back to Sunny Palms, "It was a predictable response, but at least I tried."

***

Back at Sunny Palms, Betsy and Mark prepared for the wedding. They looked through a catalogue of wedding cakes and picked out a vanilla cake with three layers, icing flowers on each layer, and a bride and groom on the top. Betsy and Mark agreed to ask the bakery to create an unclothed bride and groom on top of the cake.

They picked out wedding rings. Both were golden, and Mark's had a diamond, while Betsy's had an emerald. Then, they sent out a registry of what they wanted for wedding gifts.

***

At last, the day of the wedding arrived. Reverend Ben stood in front of the lake, between Betsy and Mark, and the guests began arriving.

Seated around the lake, as guests, were Betsy's parents, Catherine, Douglas, Mr. and Mrs. Nelson, the Barnes's with their two now-grown-up children, and various other friends Betsy had made when they came over to see her when she was in high school.

However, there was still no Laura.

Betsy sighed, and shook her head, but put her smile back on her face. She was getting married and she knew this was going to be a fabulous day.

As Mark, Betsy and the minister stood beside the lake, Mark looked Betsy in the eyes, and began to speak.

"I met this wonderful girl in a coffee shop," he began, turning his face between Betsy and the guests, "She had made a very brave decision, of coming out of the closet, of fighting the law, to live a single day to be who she is. We spoke that morning of love, compassion, and what it truly means to be human. To me, Betsy is not naked. She is clothed, but her clothing is a kind of clothing that cannot be seen with the human eye. To see Betsy's clothing, everyone, I ask you all to close your eyes. Only then, with your heart and your spirit, will you see them. Betsy's clothing is compassion, courage, happiness and unconditional love, for myself, her family, my family and for so many others. That kind of clothing of hers drew me to her, drew us closer together, day by day, every day, until here we are, at this wonderful resort, on this sunny afternoon, and I am getting married to this wonderful, young lady."

Betsy wiped a tear from her eye and spoke next, "My life has always been difficult," she wept, "my life has always been confusing. I know I am not popular with everyone in the world, but that does not stop me from loving everything and everyone, even those who do not necessarily love me. I have so much to be thankful for; my mother, my father, my sister Laura, and everyone who has dared to come forward to me, to be my friend, and that includes this wonderful man, Mark, right here. I have moved from a life shut inside my home, to a life in my back yard, to a life here with my friends, to a life here as a successful artist and bride. I thank Mark for taking me on, for seeing my true self, for accepting me as I am. His will to be my companion in life is so strong, that he has forsaken so much of what he holds dear in order to be so, and, for this, I am very thankful. For this, I gratefully take him as my husband."

The minister handed Mark and Betsy the two rings they had chosen for themselves.

Mark held the ring for Betsy, and looked Betsy in the eye, "With this ring, I take you as my wife, my loving companion, to walk with me on this Earth, for all days to come."

Mark slid the ring on Betsy's finger.

Betsy held the ring for Mark, and looked Mark in the eye, "With this ring, I take you as my husband, my loving companion, to walk with me on this Earth, for all days to come."

Betsy slid the ring on Mark's finger.

The minister spoke up.

"Do you, Mark Turner, for richer or for poorer, in sickness and in health, take Betsy Parker to be your lawfully wedded wife, till death do you part?"

Mark smiled, looked Betsy in the eyes, and said, "I do."

"Do you, Betsy Parker, for richer or for poorer, in sickness and in health, take Mark Turner to be your lawfully wedded husband, till death do you part?"

Betsy smiled, looked Mark in the eyes, and said, "I do."

"Then," smiled Reverend Ben Herb, "I now pronounce you husband and wife."

Mark and Betsy kissed. Then, together, they cheered. Every one of the guests rose from their seats and applauded.

To finalize everything, Mark and Betsy signed the certificate, and all was said and done.

A joyous reception followed that afternoon. There was food of the choicest sorts, consisting of salmon, salad, potatoes roasted in garlic, and whole-grain buns with butter. Then, the cake was cut, and presents were given.

Betsy and Mark received so many gifts that day. There was a dainty china set, a candle holder with a set of pearly white candles, a set of handmade origami swans, doves, and many other kinds of birds, and a picture of the painting of Monet's Lilly Pads.

At the end of the day, everyone was tired and well-fed, but they were all very very happy.

22 One Last Decision

Betsy was successful as an artist, surrounded by many friendly members and visitors of Sunny Palms, and married to the man she loved dearly. Betsy and Mark talked, played, worked, laughed, and enjoyed a fun, peaceful, happy life.

During Betsy and Mark's married life, many people who knew Betsy or had heard her story, were continuing the campaign for Betsy's rights. These people (family, friends, community, customers of her work, and even complete strangers) believed that Betsy should be allowed to live her life in the open, and not have to live, constantly, at Sunny Palms. Many were campaigning to police, courts, judges and magistrates on Betsy's behalf, showing their support for Betsy, and their concern that Betsy still had to live a hidden life for a condition she couldn't help.

Petitions were blooming all over the media, and polls were circulating to determine what percentage of the general public believed that Betsy should be allowed to live all the rest of her life with the rest of the world. One nationwide poll came up with a 62% “yes” response among citizens of Hilo, a 48% “yes” response from the entire state of Hawaii, and a 42% “yes” response from the USA as a whole.

When Betsy and Mark read the comments from these statistics, one particularly positive response from an Albert Duncan read, “I don't get it. We live in a day and age of equality, freedom of expression, and acceptance of differences. Despite all that, the natural human form is still regarded as taboo and needs to be hidden. People display nude works of art in public galleries all the time, with nobody objecting, but it's still a crime for an actual person to be nude in public. Betsy has never done any wrong, she has hurt no one, and she has helped so many people. To all who are against Betsy, put yourself in her shoes. Can you imagine living your life, 24-7, cradle to grave, never seeing anything except your house, or your resort? I don't care how well Betsy is accepted at Sunny Palms. If that place is all she ever sees, and the people there, the only people she ever meets, then Betsy lives in a prison, and I honestly cannot see how society prefers making Betsy live like this to letting Betsy live openly as a member of society."

A particularly negative comment from a Sally Morgan read, "What has the world come to? You ask me if Betsy Parker should be allowed to intermingle with the public like an ordinary citizen? I say 'Fine, and let's turn loose the entire population of every mental hospital, every skid-row, and let everyone intermingle with the public even if they've got the flu, the whooping cough, the measles, and every other ailment under the sun.' Hey, those people can't help being the way they are; why should we shut them away? Betsy says she wants to be acknowledged as being human. If that is so, then she can abide by human laws and human propriety and keep herself out of the public's sight. I wouldn't buy a toothpick from this Parker girl."

Despite the controversial side of Betsy Parker's issue, the protests and advocacy in Betsy's favor escalated higher into the judicial system until even the County of Hawaii was receiving letters, emails, petitions and phone calls that Betsy should be allowed to live as a normal citizen. However, every court, including the County of Hawaii, contended that it would make no proceedings unless Betsy, herself, agreed to do so.

It wasn't until eighteen months after Betsy and Mark's wedding day, after they'd had one anniversary together, when Betsy took to being quiet and withdrawn once again.

"What is it, dearest?" Mark asked her.

"I still feel left out," Betsy explained. "I make such a great living as an artist. So many people love what I make, and I am so thankful to be married to you, and to be surrounded by all these loving, happy, understanding people, but, for some reason, I am still not satisfied."

"I have been thinking the same thing," Mark explained. "I have thought about you still being shut away, and how unfair it is. It hurts me, but you've never complained, so I've never said anything about it."

"But I shouldn't feel like this," Betsy continued. "I have everything now, Mark, but I want more. I want to live a more proper human life, Mark, out in real human society, at least some of the time, even if it's just to sell my drawings and to explore the outside world once in a while. It doesn't feel right that I make the drawings, but you sell them, and I can never come face-to-face with any of the people who come to buy them."

"But sometimes, you do. Some of your customers come here."

"But that's not the same," Betsy explained. "Mark, I've settled for this much ever since the day I married you. I once thought that I would be able to settle for it forever, but it's just not working. Only some of the people who buy my work come here, and even those that do, I never get to see their faces when they see my pictures for the first time, and buy them. I want to see, first-hand, their smile, their enthusiasm, and their pleasure they must feel for my work. You are the one who does all the sales work, and it just doesn't feel right to me.

"And it's not just the artwork," Betsy continued. "I want to see more of the world. I want to see all people for who they are. I want to go places. I feel so anchored, with cabin fever, and it's really getting to me."

"I understand how you feel, for I feel it too," replied Mark. "I wish there was something I could do for you, but I can't think what. Most people in this state are not in favor of you living your life in public. The polls have shown that."

Betsy thought for a moment. "If I could only get out into, at least, the community around Sunny Palms, at least once a month, I believe that will make me content at last. I know not everyone will accept it, but I believe it will be a fair compromise between me and society. A higher percentage of people in Hilo believe I should be able to get out of Sunny Palms than the people in the rest of the state. If I can have only occasional ventures outside the resort, I think most would understand."

Mark smiled back at Betsy. "Once a month? I think that will work. We could try to lobby for all day on the last Saturday of every month. The one day you did have out in the public, when you met me, was a Saturday. On Saturdays you will probably have more customers coming to buy your work than on weekdays. You could come out and sell your work by the roadside, just like you've been wanting, while on all other days, I will keep selling your work."

"I have been thinking about that," Betsy replied. "If it's just to sell my drawings, or see the outside world, just on those occasions, that would make my life complete. Despite this, I still feel guilty; I feel ungrateful, for feeling dissatisfied and oppressed after I have accomplished so much. After all that I've accomplished, I should be satisfied. I should be proud. I should be overjoyed and thankful, and in a way I am, but in another way, I'm not, and that makes me feel all spoiled and rotten for wanting more and being dissatisfied."

"Betsy," Mark told her, with a sincere, loving smile. "You listen to me. You are neither spoiled nor rotten. You have faced a lot of difficulties, difficulties that few others on this planet can even imagine. Your feelings are normal, and the fact that you can feel this way only goes to show that you are human."

Mark looked Betsy in the face. Then, Mark turned his head and looked outside to the whole world, which stretched out far and wide.

"We'll arrange it, Betsy. Let's get your freedom."

Mark left the table, picked up a pen, and wrote a message to Judge Fred Meyer. He wrote,

Honorable Judge Meyer,

As Betsy's husband, writing on her behalf, I wish to persuade you to pass a writ to allow my wife, Betsy Alicia Parker, to have the right to be free in public as any other person, for a twenty-four-hour period on the last Saturday of every month. Betsy and myself agree that this will be so that she can have more of an opportunity to carry on a normal human life. We wish that she be allowed to live those days in the city of Hilo, without being arrested for any indecency-related offence, unless she flaunts herself, behaves lewdly, or draws undue attention to any part of her, which is something I know Betsy would never do, anyway. We urge you to consider our situation.

Mark Edward Turner and Betsy Alicia Parker

Fred Meyer agreed that it was a deep issue to be addressed as soon as possible. He sent a letter for the commencement of a hearing on February 28. Betsy, once again, would listen and communicate via video link. Mark agreed to stay at her side and communicate via video link also. Betsy's parents would be coming in person to hear and discuss the proceedings.

"Mark," smiled Betsy, once the arrangement had been made, "I have something I would like to show you. It's a picture I drew once when I was really depressed. However, when I finished drawing it, the sight of the finished work made me feel so saddened that I didn't show it to anyone. But I don't feel comfortable hiding anything, Mark, especially from you."

"Go ahead and show me," Mark replied, "I would be happy to see any art that's yours."

Betsy took her key and unlocked the drawer by the bed. She pulled the drawer open, and showed her picture to Mark, the one with her and Mark walking the grad carpet.

"Betsy!" Mark cried, when he saw the picture. "This is wonderful. You were really thinking about me, weren't you?"

"If you like it that much, you can have it," Betsy smiled.

Mark shook his head, "I don't want it," he explained. "It's gorgeous and well-drawn and all, but I suffered so much hurt and humiliation that day when I tried to walk the carpet. All it would do is remind me of the past. I want to put the past behind us, Betsy, and live life today."

"Yes," replied Betsy, "I do too," and she shut the picture back in the drawer.

***

On the day of the hearing, Betsy and Mark turned on the video link. The huge room appeared. Betsy's family was there, as well as many people from around town, most of which were complete strangers to Betsy. Some of them were holding some of Betsy's drawings. Betsy could see her parents in the front row. Justice Meyer was sitting in front of it all.

"We are here, today, to discuss a special accommodation for Betsy Parker," Meyer began. "She and her husband, Mark Turner have requested that Betsy have the same rights, once a month, on the last Saturday of every month, to be anywhere she wishes or needs to be, to explore the world in any venue where any normal-functioning person can do the same, and to not be required to spend the day at Sunny Palms. I know we are all eager to hear what will come of this, as this is a unique case, as Betsy is a unique person." Justice Meyer turned to Betsy, "We will now hear from Betsy Parker who will present her case as to why she feels this way, and what should be done to salvage this situation."

The icon of Justice Meyer in the video link turned to Betsy. "Why do you want this, Betsy?"

"Honorable Justice Meyer," she began, "I just want to say that all through my life, I have felt ostracized. I am cut off from mainstream human society, which requires all of its participants to be clothed. Justice Meyer, I only want you to understand that even I do not want to live without clothes all the time. I want to wear clothes; I really do. However, I also don't want my human rights taken away from me. I know this is hard for society to accept, but I want to be part of the human world. On several occasions throughout my life, before I found my wonderful husband, Mark, I found myself listening to the mermaid, Ariel's, song 'Part of Your World.' I felt just like Ariel, and I still do, and I will always feel that way, as long as I am shut away, treated as someone second class, who has to be hidden."

Murmurs echoed around the room. Justice Meyer's expression was sympathetic, but not conclusive.

"You must understand, Betsy, that this is a difficult decision that will require much deliberation. I am aware of the many people who have lobbied for you to have proper human rights, and in many ways, I believe they are right. However, there have been people and other groups campaigning for you to not be allowed to ever stray outside Sunny Palms. There is also the indisputable fact that you are successful. You make so many people happy, and make so much money with your artwork. You and Mark have helped so many charities with the money you have made. Also, you are married. You have a husband. Is it really fitting that a married, successful young woman, such as yourself, be allowed to parade your body around complete strangers, many of whom will be offended, many of whom will have lustful thoughts at the sight of you?"

Betsy sighed and looked thoughtful. "I do not want to parade myself," she told the courtroom in the video link, "I only want to live. I do not ask that the world be clothes-free or clothing optional for everyone. I ask for this right, for myself, only one day per month, due to an allergic condition I have through no fault of my own. If I didn't have this condition, I wouldn't be here today. I would be out in public, selling my art and exploring the world. Myself and my parents have always wanted me to be allowed to live, just as I am, ever since I had an allergic reaction all over me that nearly cost me my life when I was nine months old."

Justice Meyer faced Betsy once more, "If there are people lusting after you, and being affronted at the sight of you, will you not be, in effect, parading yourself? I have one of your watercolor paintings too, Betsy," the Judge continued, "The one that you titled 'The Love of my Life' of you and Mark together, holding hands."

"Thank you," Betsy smiled, "I am so glad you appreciate my work."

"I understand why you want more, even though you're already such a success," Meyer continued, "I also understand that if it wasn't for places such as Sunny Palms, you wouldn't have a home at all, that you would have to seek refuge with family, or the few others who would understand you. But at the end of the day, whether we're rich or poor, successful or unsuccessful, loved or hated, we all have our struggles in life, which we all have to face. We also have our blessings in life, and we must be thankful for them, and count them."

"I count my blessings every day," Betsy replied, "and I am

thankful for them all."

Justice Meyer nodded once more, "We live in a world, Betsy, that does not tolerate nakedness. One person, namely yourself, having the legal right to be naked could put a snag in the fabric of decency and modesty, a snag that might quickly unravel the rest of that fabric. There could be more people doing the same thing, Betsy, walking the streets naked, people who have no clinical condition whatsoever that prevents them from wearing clothing."

Betsy shrugged, "And so what if they are? They would be happy and free too," but the second these words had left her lips, she knew this was wrong. Not everyone would feel comfortable with it, and there would be weird people getting off on it.

"There would be people complaining, Betsy. There would be harassment going on and misfits doing unseemly things."

"I understand that," Betsy acknowledged, "and I respect that. I also understand that my situation creates a conflict within the Equal Protection Clause between equality under the law versus right to life and liberty. That is why I am not trying to sway the law to allow me to live my life in mainstream society all the time. I am trying to work for a compromise between living my life in the public and secluding myself from the public. Honorable Meyer, will you take that into consideration?"

"I will, and you are right about so much," Meyer continued, "It is human nature to not want to be hidden, to want love and acceptance, to want equality with fellow humans. However, if we were to grant you one day every month to be allowed freedom in the public, do you not worry that people will look at you inappropriately, or harass you?"

"I have thought of that," Betsy replied. "That is why I feel so conflicted about this whole situation. If I do win the right to go out, I will always be sure to have Mark at my side, hopefully my parents as well, and anyone else I know and trust who would be willing to accompany me."

"We will deliberate your situation, Betsy. It will take a while, probably at least a few weeks, for us to come to a decision. You must understand, Betsy, that this is among the most controversial cases of all time."

"I understand," Betsy acknowledged.

"Is there any more you want to say?"

"No," replied Betsy, "nothing more."

"Then I adjourn you from your part in the proceedings. We will debate the situation with your family, friends and community to determine what the overall reaction would be from a ruling in your favor, deliberate both sides, then come to a ruling."

"Thank you," Betsy and Mark smiled together. "Whatever comes of this, we will be satisfied."

The video link went dark, and Betsy's part in the trial ended.

Betsy and Mark spent some time, peacefully together, alone in their home on Sunny Palms.

"Well, that's that, Betsy," Mark smiled. "We tried. At least we can be proud of that. It's because you're so successful. For once, perhaps it would have been better if you had remained unemployed and never got married. Maybe, that would have helped the case to work in your favor."

"No," Betsy smiled. "It wouldn't have. The proceedings and the ruling wouldn't have been any different. He's right. We all have our difficulties, and we must face them."

"You're right," Mark replied.

"Mark," Betsy smiled, "Whatever the Judge rules in this case, I will still be grateful that I was granted that one day of freedom to go out and find you."

23 A Walk of Hope

It wasn't until three weeks later when Justice Fred Meyer made his decision. Since Betsy had spoken over the video link, a case had proceeded that involved Carl and Megan telling the story of Betsy's life complete with her struggles and her victories. Kyle and Emma Barnes had spoken about how they had routinely played with Betsy at her house since she was three, that it was fun, that she had become a friend to them, and that it had been no different from playing with any other childhood friend.

The case had sprung up online, and on televisions, magazines and newspapers all over the country. The whole time, Mark and Betsy had been following, intently, on what the verdict would be.

On March 21, Justice Meyer announced, "Now that all parties have been called and both sides of the case have been deliberated thoroughly, we have decided that Betsy's having a twenty-four-hour period on the last Saturday of every month is a fair solution to her situation. On these days, and on only these days, Betsy Parker will be immune from charges for simple nudity and nothing more. It is expected, on these days, that Betsy will meet her customers, in person, as they purchase her artwork, and that Betsy will take walks in the area near Sunny Palms, possibly meeting or talking to some of her fellow people of the city along the way.

"As we are aware of the possible repercussions of this ruling, there will be some restrictions: Betsy must always remain within the city of Hilo, and she must not venture onto or into the premises of, or in view of, a daycare centre, a playground, a preschool, elementary school or high school, or a church or other place of religious worship. Betsy must also understand that this remains a situation open to further protests and challenges from those opposing her. If these protests become too strong or too many, it remains possible that we will revoke this privilege we are bestowing upon her. Until that time, if any, I hereby adjourn the proceedings. May Betsy be allowed to venture as she will starting on Saturday, March 30."

A wave of delight swept through Betsy that was so intense it left her speechless. After a silence in which she savored this miraculous ruling, she regained her words. Betsy, this time, did not cry out, but instead, whispered, slowly and dreamily, "This is just what I have always wanted. I don't know what to say. I can't believe this is even real."

Despite Betsy's awe-struck delight and amazement, Mark remained unsatisfied, "You can't go anywhere near a school? There are children right here at Sunny Palms. You were once a child yourself, with a body not unlike any of those children who go to school. And no church for you either? What if, at some point, you decide you want to join a church?"

"Mark," Betsy assured him, "Whatever other parents do not want their children to see, or be exposed to, I have no problem honoring that. Besides, I don't have to go to church. This whole world is God's place. I live in a church. No manmade building, designed to worship God, could be more important to me than this resort and this Earth."

With Betsy's last statement, Mark's expression turned into a smile, once more, as well. "You know Betsy? You are right, and I am happy for you. This is a unique privilege. No one else in the world has this right you have been granted. We should be proud. On March 30 we will go out."

***

When March 30 arrived, the sky was clear and the sun shone as

Betsy and Mark awoke that morning. They ate breakfast, showered, and let the sun dry them.

"This is it," Mark smiled. "Let's go out and see the great beyond once again."

Betsy and Mark walked across the grounds side-by-side, and proceeded towards the gate. There, at the gate, were a group of people already awaiting Betsy and Mark's arrival: Carl, Megan, Catherine, and, much to Betsy's delight, surprise, and amazement ... Laura!

"Oh Laura!" Betsy cried. "I haven't seen you for so long! It's wonderful to see you again."

"It's wonderful to see you too, Betsy," Laura smiled. "Betsy, I have been thinking lately. I've been a dreadful sister. I've dismissed you, walked out on you, and done pretty well everything I could to get you out of my life. But I love you, Betsy. I'm proud of you, and everything you have done. I've given a lot of thought about what I have been doing to you, and have decided to come back to you, to apologize. Can you ever forgive me?"

"Laura," Betsy smiled, "of course I forgive you. I could never have wished for a better sister. Come on Laura. Come on everyone. Let's head out."

Betsy, Mark, Catherine, Carl, Megan and Laura stepped out the gate of Sunny Palms into the sunshine, as the warm air and a soft breeze cuddled them all. Everyone, except for Betsy, was clothed but that didn't matter to Betsy.

"It's a gorgeous day," smiled Catherine. "It's been raining a lot lately, and I was worried it wouldn't be such a great day to go out."

Megan spoke next. "I would go out any day," she smiled, "Rain or shine, any day for my Betsy."

Carl turned to Betsy. "I am so proud of you dear, taking the initiative to go to court to get your human rights. Good for you."

After the six had walked on a little ways, Laura spoke again. "I have a new boyfriend," she told Betsy. "His name is Antonio. I met him at my new school. I think he's a better match, much better than Carlos. I've told Antonio all about you. He thinks you're great."

"Well that's terrific Laura," Betsy smiled. "I am so proud of you."

"Next month when we go out, I am planning on bringing Antonio," Laura continued. "He would like to meet you."

"That's great, Laura. I would like to meet him too."

"I think it was Antonio that made me decide to come back to you. I was alone after leaving my previous school. Then, I met this wonderful young man at my new school, who made me feel so much better. Then, I realized that must be how life is like for you, Betsy. You were all alone, but then you met Mark, and life became better for you. I thought about how I had been treating you, and chose to come back, to be your sister once again."

"Do you think you will come back to Sunny Palms?" Betsy asked.

Laura sighed. "I will definitely come to visit you, but I wouldn't be able to stay for long. I don't think I would ever be able to go there unclothed again. I would feel too exposed, self-conscious, and vulnerable. But I'm sure Susan would understand if I came clothed, and visited you for a few hours one day here and there. I promise to come with you every time you venture out of Sunny Palms on the last Saturday of every month."

"Thank you Laura," Betsy smiled. "That would make my life complete."

Mark started thumbing around in his pocket. He pulled out the picture Betsy had drawn of him and Betsy at grad.

"You don't mind if I show this to Laura, do you?" Mark asked Betsy.

"Why no, go ahead," Betsy replied.

"Betsy drew this," Mark explained to Laura. "She felt so sad about not being with me at my high school graduation that she drew it." He put the picture in Laura's hands, and Laura took hold of it.

As Laura eyed it, an intrigued expression crossed her face. "I like it," she smiled, facing Betsy. "It catches you, Mark, and everyone else perfectly. May I buy it from you?"

"You can have it for free," Betsy smiled at Laura. "You're my sister, and I don't need any money for this picture. I will gladly give it to you."

"Thank you," Laura smiled back. "I think I'll call it 'A Walk of Hope.' Does that sound like a good title?"

"That sounds like a great title," Betsy replied. "In fact, I wouldn't be able to think of anything better."

Betsy set 'A Walk of Hope' in Laura's hands, and Laura took it. Laura looked it over with an expression of joy, feeling so proud of Betsy.

"And Betsy?" Laura continued.

"Yes?"

"Thank you for helping me with my homework."

"You are very welcome, Laura."

The six turned right at the next intersection, and they continued walking down a longer road where grass grew on either side. They kept walking, nobody saying a word, everyone enjoying the peace, the quiet and the fresh air.

Finally, the road ended in a peaceful, grassy meadow. There was birdsong in the trees, the sound of the wind in the grass, and in the middle of this meadow was a pond with lily pads, and a fountain in the middle of the pond.

Betsy was lost in awe.

"This is gorgeous," she breathed at last, "so beautiful, so

peaceful, so quiet."

She stopped talking, stood in silence, and closed her eyes, savoring the texture of the air on her skin, feeling the breeze, and taking in the sounds and smells of this scene.

After a long time of peace and quiet, Betsy turned back to her friends and family. "I love this place," she smiled. "I love you all. I love everyone, and I love myself."

Her father smiled at Betsy. "That is wonderful Betsy. You know, so do I. It's good to love."

"And I love my body," Betsy continued, "and I love every part of it. Every part of my body is a precious friend to me, helping me to live and be happy, and there is no part of it I have any ill thoughts or feelings towards or am ashamed of. Humankind is one big body, and I am part of it."

By now, all five of the people accompanying Betsy were crying. "Betsy," her mother wept. "That is so beautiful. You have made my whole day, just now."

"I am ready to head back," Betsy smiled. "I don't need to be out here all day. I've seen all I want to see, and done all I want to do. I am ready to go back to the home I love."

The six explorers made their way back. Once more, everyone was silent as they walked along the road from the meadow. They turned left onto the main road to make their way back to Sunny Palms.

They had only begun their walk on the main road, when a black lab dashed onto the side. A passing car swerved to avoid hitting the dog, and, as a result, the car came roaring on towards two pedestrians.

In the split second that followed, Betsy and Mark realized who these pedestrians were. They were Mark's parents, walking home from their Saturday afternoon Bible study group at the church.

Betsy dashed forward, and Mark followed, running just a foot behind her. Betsy got to Mr. and Mrs. Turner first and pushed them out of the way. Mark, who was just behind, was still in danger of being hit. Betsy pushed him onto the roadside, and prepared to dash out of the way of the car to save herself, but it was too late.

The car struck Betsy, and she went flying across the road, and landed, in a bloody mess down the street.

The world reeled in front of Mark's eyes. All in a nanosecond, everything blurred, then came back into focus, and he saw Betsy.

“BETSY!!!” he cried. Mark, Laura, Catherine, Carl and Megan all ran up to Betsy.

By the time they reached her, she was no longer breathing, and a dark red, purple, blistery anaphylactic rash was spreading all over her.

“Don't worry Betsy!” hollered Mark, as he whipped his phone out of his pocket and called 911. “I'm getting an ambulance for you. They will get you to the hospital. You are going to be okay!”

Mark looked over his shoulder. What were his parents doing now? Betsy had just saved their lives at her own cost. Would they have the grace, at least, to come forward to see if she was okay? The car that had hit her hadn't stopped, either. It had vanished out of sight. Mark's parents were taking each other by the hands, and walking away in the opposite direction, retreating down the side of the road. Fury burned inside Mark. It was a hit and run, he was losing his wife, and his parents didn't even care.

“AAAAAAAAAAAAAAHHHHHHHHHH!!!” Mark hollered, and began to give breaths to Betsy, holding her nose, breathing into her mouth, anything to keep her alive.

“My dear,” Betsy's mother wept, as she kneeled at Betsy's side. “I'm here. I love you. Don't worry. I will always be here for you.”

For what seemed like an eternity, Mark continued trying to

resuscitate Betsy, who no longer showed any signs of life, and had a horrible rash all over her body. The rash, in and of itself, was severe enough to be deadly, even if she hadn't been hit.

At last, the ambulance arrived. Two paramedics stepped out and looked Betsy over.

"So, Betsy Parker again," one of them said. "Come on, sweetheart. We will take you to the hospital."

Betsy gave one last, struggling, gasping breath. Then, she lay still.

"Is that it?" the medic's partner asked.

They both looked the girl over. They checked her pulse, checked her breathing and all other vital signs.

"That's it," sighed the first paramedic. "She's gone."

24 A Comforting Message

Mark was in complete disbelief and denial. He couldn't take in that this had really happened. He must be hallucinating, or dreaming, or deluded from the heat, but Betsy hadn't died. She couldn't have. It was impossible, not his happy, sweet, loving, wonderful Betsy. He looked around at all the others. Every one of them had a shocked, upset, grieving expression, but Mark's tears felt like they would never end.

"We will take you," one of the paramedics called. "We are both very sorry about this, but we will take you all to the hospital, where you can see Betsy."

"No!" Mark exclaimed. "I've always seen Betsy as a living, wonderful girl. I couldn't stand to see her dead!"

Mark turned, once more, to his four companions on the roadside to see what they would do.

Carl and Megan turned to Mark, and they both gave a sigh of mingled grief and comfort. "We'll go see Betsy," Carl explained. "We will go to the hospital and see her, while we have the chance to."

"What will you do, Laura?" Mark asked.

"I'll go with my parents. She was my sister, Mark. Are you sure you don't want to go? She was your wife."

"Was! Was!" Mark cried. "I can't bear to hear that word. I can't see her, not dead. I just can't."

And Mark turned to walk away.

Catherine followed after him. "I'll walk with you," she explained. "Betsy was my best friend, a gentle soul, and I'm really going to miss her. I want to go and see her too, but I also don't want you to be alone, and Betsy wouldn't either. Come on. Let's walk together."

As the Parkers departed in the ambulance, Mark and Catherine walked along the roadside.

Mark trembled as he walked, but his tears had slowed.

"Thank you Catherine," Mark wept. "Thank you for thinking of me, but I loved Betsy, and I can't live without her."

"Mark," Catherine reassured him, as she wiped a tear from her own cheek. "Things will get better for you, I promise. Things will get better for all of us. I am heartbroken at losing Betsy, but I know, deep down, that I will come to accept what has happened and live on. Someday, you will too."

"But Betsy wasn't just any wife," Mark wept. "She was the one person who touched me deep down, who made me humble, who made me laugh, who made me understand that there are more important things in the world besides the clothes we wear."

"Betsy is still with you," Catherine soothed, beginning to smile. "She is still with all of us. She left a deep mark on us all, the whole of humanity possibly, but she is not lost. You'll always be able to feel her presence, her voice in your heart, whenever you are quiet and calm."

Mark remained silent. He tried to calm himself, but the grief, shock and loss he felt would not go away. Betsy had died, and he was never going to see her again.

After they had walked a little further, Mark spoke up again. "It's all my fault," he said.

"What's your fault?"

"It's my fault she died. I didn't get out of the way of that car fast enough, and Betsy had to stay behind to push me out of the way. Besides, those were my parents, those cold, unfeeling creatures who threw me out of their home, and never felt any compassion, whatsoever, for Betsy. I shouldn't have tried to save them in the first place. What was I thinking?"

"Mark," Catherine assured him, "None of this is your fault. You won't get anywhere if you blame yourself. It's tragic, but you were doing your duty, when you rushed to save your parents, and so was Betsy. She didn't need to do that, Mark. Your parents were so awful that day at the gate that I wouldn't have blamed her if she hadn't, but she loved everyone that much. She was such a selfless person that she put the needs of those cold, nasty parents of yours above her own, and saved them. You think of that, Mark. You remember that about her. Betsy is a person worthy of remembering. Mark, however your parents react to being saved is their decision alone."

"Hey Catherine," Mark breathed, his tears finally dissipating. "You referred to Betsy as 'is.'"

"That's right Mark, I did, because she will never be gone. She's gone into another world, Mark, that's all, a world where she is truly happy, loved and accepted."

"I know, Catherine," Mark wept. "I know, but that's not the way I can see things, not now."

Mark and Catherine walked on a little ways further.

"Take me to my parents," said Mark. "I want a word with them."

"Yeah, okay," Catherine replied.

***

When Mark arrived at his parents' house, he pounded on the door.

"Let me in!" Mark hollered. "Now!"

"There's nobody home," came the voice of his father from inside.

"Oh yes there is!" Mark demanded, "and I want in!"

"Now now Brian," came the voice of Mrs. Turner, "Mark's here. Let's go see what all this is about."

Mark's mother opened the door, and Mark stared deep into her eyes, glaring with hatred and contempt of this filthy monster of a mother who was looking back at him.

"She saved your lives!" Mark hollered loudly enough so that both his parents would hear. "She saved your lives, and sacrificed herself, and there you were walking home from your church Bible study group as if nothing happened, and here you are still acting indifferent to me and to what Betsy did for you, and you don't have the strength or the gall to say a word about me or her, and you have no thoughts, feelings or anything towards me, towards her friend Catherine, or towards her parents and sister who were left behind!"

"Mark!" his father called from the kitchen. "She saved us, yes. But do you really think that redeems the fact that she was-"

"There was nothing that needed to be redeemed!" Mark yelled. "She was perfect the way she was, and I could never have had a better wife, not even in my dreams! You're right dad! You were perfectly right when you said 'God would never create a person who has to be an exhibitionist in order to live' because Betsy was no exhibitionist! She was a wonderful person and we loved each other!"

"She died on scene," his mother cried, "What could we have done? There was nothing more we could have done then."

"OH ... YES ... THERE ... WAS!!!" Mark yelled from the doorway, for he couldn't bear to come inside this ghastly place. "SHE WAS DYING AND YOU TOOK NO RESPONSIBILITY, SHOWED NO COMFORT, NO REMORSE ... ***NOTHING!!!!!***

"AND YOU KNOW WHAT?" Mark hollered. "I'M NOT EVEN TALKING TO YOU ANYMORE. I'LL NEVER SPEAK TO YOU, SEE YOU, OR THINK OF YOU AGAIN. ***I*** AM

DISOWNING ***YOU***. HOW DO YOU LIKE THAT?"

SLAM!

After Mark had slammed the door, he ran away from the house to get as far away as he possibly could from this place.

"Just get me out of here, Catherine," he breathed. "Hurry!"

***

That night, Mark couldn't sleep. The room was cold, spooky and empty without Betsy. The grief of losing her, and the bitter hatred Mark felt towards his parents burned inside him. He tossed and turned hour after hour, but he felt like he was thrashing in a mud puddle in a cold, bleak cave.

At some point or another, for Mark neither knew nor cared what time it was, Mark got out of bed, got dressed, and walked away. He didn't know where. He didn't know when he'd stop. He just wanted to get away from everything, away from everyone, away from the world.

It was a sensation Mark had never encountered before. He had gotten so used to Betsy for comfort. Numerous times, during the period when he knew her, both before and during their married life, Mark would get depressed about something, or something wouldn't go right, but there was Betsy, with her loving smile, soft words, and sparkling eyes, always there to comfort him, and Mark would feel better right away.

But now, there was no Betsy to comfort him. This was one of his moments he could have used Betsy's comfort the most. Alas, here Mark was; depressed, grief-stricken, angry and alone, with no one to turn to.

He walked and walked until he found a large rock, where he sat down. Once seated upon the rock, Mark gazed into the starry sky.

He sat in silence and felt the night all around him. The nighttime was a void that surrounded him. The air was still warm from the daylight, but Mark shivered. He sat motionless on the rock, listening to nothing except his own breath, that one sound that kept him company, the sound that was himself, the only person he had left.

But Mark could not live like that, not alone.

Betsy's price to give Mark the gift of life had been herself. Alas, here Mark was, alive because of Betsy, the angel for whom Mark would have gladly given his own life to save. It had been her one final act of goodness that accompanied all her other virtues, which, to Mark, outnumbered the hairs on her head. The rest of Mark's life was a gift from Betsy, but it was a gift he found himself unable to accept, for in this gift Betsy had given him, she was not there.

Betsy's price to give Mark's parents the gift of redemption had been herself. Alas, in that gift of redemption, there was no acceptance, no thanks, no reciprocation. The hearts of Mark's parents were so cold and so hardened that nothing Betsy did mattered to them. In their hearts, there was no love, but only pretence, blindness and hypocrisy. In their eyes, the sole fact that Betsy could never wear any clothes cancelled out, and rendered null and void, everything she did.

Mark's solitude grew darker and darker, as his loss and despair were dragging him deeper and deeper into that cold, bleak cave, until all light was blotted out.

Then, he reached a point where he sat in impenetrable blackness. He was beyond grief stricken, beyond hopeless, beyond reproach; he felt dead. Everything that had given Mark hope had been sucked out of him, and he felt like a skeleton sitting on that lonely rock, separated from his body and the world, never to rise again.

At the final instant, when Mark had arrived at this deepest, darkest point, and there was no further to go, a feeling of euphoria swept over him. It was indescribable. It was happiness, love, joy, peace, and so many more bright, happy, wonderful feelings all bubbling in him at once. He felt a pair of arms wrapping themselves around him, comforting him, holding him, like a mother holding her newborn baby. They were arms of a quality he had never felt before, the arms of an angel. An all-loving, pure, white, benevolent, laughing, joyous angel was holding him, loving him, comforting him.

He could sense a playful laugh in his heart. He couldn't hear it, at least not in the way people of this world normally hear, but he could sense it, like it was being sent to a kind of extra sense he never knew he had.

Mark looked all around him. He saw no one, but he could feel someone, someone very special. Betsy was there. It was that one presence that he truly knew. Mark was not alone; he could feel Betsy sitting there with him, smiling, laughing, loving him, comforting him.

"It is not time, precious one," came Betsy's voice in the same way her laugh had come, "You are not ready. You have more to accomplish. Come away. Come away, back to this world. Let go of all that troubles you. Have no anger, no hatred, no grudges. Live in peace. Live, laugh, learn, love, and always be at peace."

The presence left him, but the feelings it left within him remained. Mark sat up from the rock. A tear rolled out of his eye, then another, then one from the other eye, and Mark dropped onto the ground and began to cry tears of joy, comfort and peace. He felt guilty for not feeling thankful for the rest of his life, but that guilt was washed away by the euphoric feelings he now had. After some time, Mark cried himself to sleep.

25 A Comforting Place

When Mark awoke, it was another bright and sunny morning. He was a little surprised to find himself in the open glade, but he awoke with a new sense of eagerness, determination and joy.

Mark decided, right then, that the first thing he would do would be to rebuild the broken bridge between himself and his parents. Before now, he never thought he would be able to do this, that he didn't even want to. Now, Mark felt that it was his duty, his priority, to honor the memory of Betsy Parker. He would knock on their door, and visit them every day. Every day, he would sit inside their house, talk maybe, then see if maybe, yet, his parents would accept him, once more, as their son.

Mark vowed to see Roger too. However cold and callous Roger was, they were still brothers, still a family, and Mark still had him.

Mark rose and walked back to Sunny Palms. He dressed, made some breakfast, and left the resort to pay his parents a visit.

"Where are you going, Mark?" Catherine asked when she saw him.

"I'm going to visit my parents," Mark replied.

"Are you serious? They were so horrible to you yesterday, and you said yourself that you never wanted to see them again."

"I've come to feel I need to," Mark replied. "I cannot guarantee that I can rebuild anything with them, but the least I can do is to try, and then I'll be happy that I tried. Besides, today is Easter Sunday, and there couldn't be any better way to celebrate this day than by resurrecting relationships."

"Good for you Mark," Catherine beamed. "That is what I like to hear. I'll come with you."

Mark shook his head. “Thank you Catherine,” he replied, “but no. I think it's better that I do this myself.”

Catherine nodded. “Okay Mark. Good luck, and happy Easter.”

“Happy Easter, Catherine,” Mark smiled in return.

Mark left the resort, and before he knew it, he was at his parents' door. Mark knocked gently, rather than the pounding he had made the previous day.

The door opened. There was his father at the other side.

“Oh, it's you again,” Mr. Turner snarled. “I thought you'd disowned us. Well, we disowned you first. Goodbye.”

Mark's father slammed the door.

“No! Wait!” cried Mark. “Please let me in; just for five minutes.”

The door creaked open one more time.

“Okay, if that's what you want. Five minutes it is then, but I can't see what brings you back here.”

“Thank you so much,” Mark smiled.

He stepped onto the landing, removed his shoes, and stepped up the stairs. Mark's father sat down, once more, at the breakfast table with Mark's mother, and Mark sat in what used to be his own chair at the table.

Mark sat there the whole time, just sitting, silent, with his parents. He didn't even tell them the amazing encounter and the message he had felt the previous night. He sat there, without ever saying a word, letting his parents take in his thoughts, his feelings, his presence.

When the five minutes were up, Mark rose from the table.

“Thanks for letting me in,” Mark smiled. “That was all I wanted. Bye for now.”

And Mark left.

The next day, Mark came to his parents' house for ten minutes, again saying nothing the whole time, just sitting with them at the kitchen table.

The next day, Mark came for fifteen minutes. By now, his parents were really wondering what was going on. Twelve minutes into the fifteen, Mark's father asked, “Mark, are you okay? What is this you're doing?”

“I just want to see you,” Mark replied. “I just want a little quiet time with you. That's all.”

Every day, Mark added five more minutes onto his stays at his parents' house. A week into his daily visits, Mark and his parents began engaging in conversation once more.

“You really want to love us, don't you Mark?” his mother asked him.

“I do,” Mark replied. “And I don't want to love you. I do love you. But I loved Betsy too. Is there something wrong with that? Can't I love whoever I choose?”

At this, both of Mark's parents retreated into silence. They were confused and baffled. How could Mark love them, when he also loved Betsy?

The visits continued. On the twelfth day, the visits came to an hour, and an hour was how long they stayed. There was mostly silence exchanged at these visits, with Mark hoping his parents would sit quietly, thinking about who their son really was; hoping, just hoping that maybe, one day, they would understand Betsy for who she had really been, and honor her name.

After two weeks, Mark's parents opened up enough to discuss one person who had long been absent from Mark's life.

“Roger has been arrested,” his father explained. “We've known this for several days now, Mark, but we've never told you. He's been charged with hit and run. It was him who was driving the car that killed Betsy. He was driving to pick Xavier up from his friend Marco's house at the time of the crash."

Mark was stunned. The wind was knocked out of him. "It was Roger?" he gasped. "Do you know this, or is it only suspected?"

"We know it," Mark's mother sighed. "The police stopped him further down the road, got his license number and took him into custody. He's in jail now, awaiting trial."

"Then we're going to see Roger!" Mark called. "Mom! Dad! Are you coming?"

"You bet we are!" Mark's dad called. "Come on, son. Let's go."

The three bundled into Mark's parents' car and drove to the county jail. When they got there, there was Roger, in a waiting cell.

"Roger!" Mark sobbed, when he saw his brother. "Was it really you? Did you run over Betsy?"

"I did," Roger admitted. "At first I thought, 'It's just that naked freak. She's not even a proper person. I don't need to stop for her,' but further down the road, my conscience, the conscience I haven't felt for many years, seized me. I felt a sense of grief and guilt I hadn't felt in a long time. It came to light that I really had run over a human being, possibly killed her, and that I had driven away. I was further troubled when it dawned on me that she had saved mom and dad, and I would have stopped for mom and dad right away if I had hit them. Rochelle has left me, and is planning to file for divorce. She picked Xavier up after I got arrested, phoned me and told me our life together was over. She says I'm a bad example for Xavier. She doesn't want Xavier to grow up with a hit and run driver for a father."

"Roger," Mark breathed in amazement and wonder. "You actually feel badly about what you did? I can't express how I feel, and I don't think I have ever seen you show remorse for anything."

Roger continued. "When I was further down the road, my

feelings of guilt became so strong, that I decided to turn around to see if Betsy was okay, but that was the point when the police found me and busted me. They informed me she had died, and I felt terrible."

Mark's mother and father smiled at their older son. Mark did too.

"Brother," Mark reassured Roger. "It's going to be okay. I'll come to visit you in prison often, I promise. I forgive you, Roger."

"Mark," Mrs. Turner smiled. "Good for you for wanting to see Roger once again. Roger, good for you for deciding to help."

"Nice to see you, sonny," Mr. Turner winked at Roger. "Mark's right. We will all be visiting you regularly."

Mark was blown away. He had never seen anything like this before. Here he was, having a peaceful conversation with his whole family. He didn't know what to make of it.

***

The day of Betsy's funeral arrived. The church was crammed, with all space on every pew taken, and many people were standing. Everyone carried a solemn, mournful expression, and a good many were wiping their eyes with handkerchiefs. Carl, Megan, Laura, Antonio, Mark and Catherine were sitting in the front pew, and Minister Jane Jordan was standing at the front.

"We gather, today, to commemorate the life of Betsy Alicia Parker," she began. "In her twenty-one years of life, from January 16 1992 to March 30 2013, Betsy touched so many. In all her years, she could never wear any clothes, but she lit up the atmosphere everywhere she went, and wherever she was, there was never a sad face. We mourn her loss, but we remember her, celebrate her life, and carry on with our own lives. Betsy Parker may have left us in person, but she is still with us all in spirit."

Jane proceeded to tell the congregation the story of Betsy's life, all the way from her birth to the events leading up to her death. Then, she called Betsy's family to the front to give her eulogy.

Mark was the first to rise and step forward. "I met you in a coffee shop," he began, in a contemplative, meditating voice. "From that day onward, I loved you. You weren't just my friend. You were never just my friend. You were my companion, my life, and my loving, wonderful wife. Thank you, Betsy. Thank you for everything. Thank you for putting a smile on my face every day, for being yourself, and for saving my parents. All your life, you sought acceptance. You sought to be loved, and to be treated at the same level as your fellow people of this planet, and now you have that. You have finally found a place where you are loved, happy, and accepted in every conceivable way. I look up to you every day, in hopes that I can be more like you: happy, kind, energetic, loving, forgiving, humble, modest, unselfish, friendly, and good, and some day I will join you in that special place you have found yourself."

Mark wiped his eyes one more time, and stepped down from the pulpit. Laura was the next to stand at the front. She was carrying Betsy's picture 'A Walk of Hope.'

"I wasn't always there for you Betsy," she said in a soft voice. "I wasn't always comfortable with you, or what you were, but now, I see the error of my ways. You were my sister, Betsy, my beloved sister, and you still are. We played together as little girls and had so much fun. Now, I cherish those days, and wish, with all my heart, that I could have them back; that you could be here and we could live those days all over again. If only I had seen more of your life, seen your wedding, seen you fight for your rights. If I had only smiled at you as you left on that plane to Hawaii. Now, I miss you, but I will remember you by the wonderful artwork you gave the world. I am thankful, Betsy, so thankful that I got to see you one last time."

Laura's boyfriend, Antonio, gave his eulogy next. "I wish I could have met you, Betsy. I met your sister, Laura, at school. Laura told me about you. Our conversation continued into an in-depth discussion about your life, and I was fascinated by the various ways your life had played out. Then, Laura promised to return to you. I told Laura that I wanted to meet you, after Laura had had one more visit with you, but your life came to a close, from performing one final act of unconditional love. Now that I have heard all about you, I promise to do all I can to honor you."

Betsy's parents made their eulogy next, and Betsy's father spoke.

"When Betsy was born, my wife and I were happy and intrigued that The Lord had sent us a healthy, beautiful baby girl. We were even happier when she began to develop and grow like any ordinary baby. We fed her, bathed her, clothed her, changed her diapers,"

A few people laughed at this point.

"but when it was revealed that our daughter had a unique condition that kept her from wearing any clothing at all, or touching pretty-well anything with any portion of her skin apart from her mouth, hands, and feet, my wife and I were horrified and dumbstruck. We didn't know what we were going to do with our daughter. We were afraid she would accidentally have a giant allergic reaction, which would kill her in her infancy, but, worst of all, we were afraid that our daughter would live her whole life, whatever it was going to be, as a hermit and an invalid, never meeting any people, never knowing anyone, never learning or exploring, and never being loved, understood, or appreciated, by anyone except my wife and me."

At this point, Megan took over. "Now, we both know that our daughter lived, and she lived a grand life, despite our fear, for she grew into a successful, smart, talented young woman. She was loved by us, by her husband, by the other campers at Sunny Palms and by the many people who came to buy her art, whether in person or online. I am proud to have been the mother of this delightful girl, and my husband, Carl, is proud to have been her father. Rest in peace Betsy, and may no one ever doubt you again."

Catherine was the last to step to the front and speak.

"I am not saying we should all be nudists," she began. "There are billions of people on this planet that would never set foot in a nudist resort, campground, event or venue of any kind. But that doesn't mean that they are any less noble, any less worthy, any less intelligent, or any less kind, than my friend, Betsy. I was raised as a nudist by my parents, and I had the pleasure of meeting Betsy Parker, for the first time, at Sunny Palms, when she was seven and I was eight. We played together, laughed together and had so much fun together. She was a real delight in my life, a bubble, a gem, and I don't think I would be as happy as I am right now, if I had never met her."

A reception followed the service. In a side room of the church, a table was laden with sandwiches, fruits, sweets, pastries, and other tasty eats. As Mark picked up an egg sandwich, he noticed a group of young men walking towards him: his former friends from school.

"Hey Mark," Peter began in a mournful, apologetic voice. "That was a wonderful eulogy you made. It brought tears to my eyes. We came to Betsy's funeral to tell you that we are all very sorry we teased you in the cafeteria."

Sebastian spoke up next. "The day we heard about the crash, and that she had died saving your parents, we felt terrible that you had lost your wife, and even more sorry about the way we had treated you for forming a relationship with her. Sounds like you loved her a lot."

"I did," Mark smiled, turning to his friends, "and I still do. I can still feel Betsy's presence in my heart and spirit. Thank you for your apology. I am glad to have you as my friends again."

"I've been wanting to buy something of Betsy's for some time," Tony explained. "When word about Betsy started going around, I looked up what she had made and it was stunning, but I didn't want to buy anything because I had laughed at her, and I couldn't get over the idea that someone like Betsy could do all that."

"She could do all that and a whole lot more," Mark told him. "I will remain her sales partner, and sell all that I can to honor her. Whatever you want to buy, that Betsy made, is yours."

At the end of the funeral, the Parkers, Antonio, Catherine, Mark and all the guests left the church. Now, Mark knew that life was going to get better for him. Since that day at the funeral, Carl, Megan, Laura, Antonio, Mark and Catherine formed a pact, swearing to do everything they could to honor Betsy's name. They used the money Betsy and Mark had made from selling art to open a museum, called "The World in the Eyes of Betsy Parker" specifically for the purpose of displaying Betsy's art. It was located in the centre of the city, and everyone, whenever the museum was open, was welcome to come and pay to see what Betsy had made. The six arranged for a bench to be constructed near the museum entrance that bared a plaque, featuring Betsy's name. Sunny Palms was renamed to commemorate Betsy as well, and the new name was 'Betsy's Resort.'

Roger pleaded guilty to the charge of the hit and run death of Betsy, was sentenced to ten years in jail, and lost his driver's license permanently. Once a month, on the last Saturday of every month, Mark and his parents visit Roger. They talk about Roger's possibilities for his re-integration into society, the legacy Betsy left, and how the lives of Mark and the rest of his pact are playing out. Mark's parents still disapprove of the fact that their son has become a nudist, and they still haven't made a real apology about how they treated Betsy, or treated Mark for forming a relationship with her, but they accept Mark's presence whenever they go to visit Roger.

Mark sees Xavier as well. Rochelle is raising him, with the help of her parents and Mark. Mark is charmed by Xavier and impressed at what a sweet, playful, wonderful boy he is becoming. Xavier is now six years old, and Mark comes over from time to time to play with him. Mark, atop being a museum worker, and spending much time with the Parkers and Catherine, considers this a great honor. He cares for Xavier regularly, and is pleased that the little boy finally has a decent childhood.

"You want to play puppets?" Mark asked the little boy one day, while looking after him.

"Puppets?" laughed Xavier. "I love puppets."

They proceeded to make finger puppets out of cut-out pieces of felt, glue, and googly eyes.

"Hey, I'm much bigger than you," cried one of Mark's puppets to Xavier's.

"So?" cried the little boy. "I've got your nose," and Xavier clamped his fingers tightly around Mark's pointer.

"Aaaaaaggghhh, he's got me!" Mark cried, and then Mark laughed.

Later, Mark and Rochelle brought Xavier into the back yard. They brought out children's finger paints and painted what they saw around them. Mark painted himself, Rochelle painted herself, and Xavier painted himself as a little stick-boy. Then, Xavier painted a tree on either side and a giant bird overhead, big enough to knock the trees down.

"Hey, that's a big bird!" Mark laughed.

"And he's coming to get you, uncle Mark!" Xavier laughed back.

At the end of August of that year, just before Labor Day, Mr. and Mrs. Parker, Laura, Antonio, Mark and Catherine embarked on a special vacation.

"Where are we going?" Mark asked Mrs. Parker.

"You will see when we get there," she replied.

They packed their belongings, drove to the airport, boarded a plane and took off.

"I like flying on an airplane," Laura smiled. "It has windows, rows of seats, a full crew, and everything."

An hour into the flight, the crew served everyone lunch.

"And food too!" Laura cried, taking a bite of a salmon sandwich.

When the plane landed, the six stepped out onto a cooler, but still reasonably warm, late-summer landscape. The air was peaceful and carried a mellow quality, indicating that autumn was just around the corner. Some of the leaves were turning as well.

Mark looked at Catherine who carried an intrigued, curious, interested smile. They carried their luggage out of the airport, and walked around town until they came to a quiet, peaceful, sunny park.

"Where is this?" Mark asked. "Wherever it is, it sure is a pretty place."

Megan smiled. "This is Lilly Park, the park in Betsy's home town of Meriton, where my husband and I met for the first time."

"I love it," Mark smiled back. "I have never seen anything like this before. How did Betsy like living around here?"

"She adored it," Megan breathed, her voice slow, smooth and content.

"Then I adore it too," replied Mark in a similar voice.

"Come on," Carl smiled. "Let's go bask under that big Beech Tree over there."

"You're on, dear," his wife replied.

"I met your mother here, Laura," explained Carl, turning to his daughter. "I met her right here in this very park, under this very tree."

"That's wonderful, dad," smiled Laura. "I'm so glad you met Megan, and had Betsy and me."

The six walked over to the tree, and sat down, all around the base of its trunk, under its sheltering branches.

For a long time, nobody said another word. They sat there, breathing, quiet, relaxing in the shade, with the warm sun all around them, sometimes gazing into the branches, sometimes listening to the song of the birds, sometimes taking in a long draft of the sweet air, on this mellow evening on August 31.

Afterword

I began to write "The Sheltered Life of Betsy Parker" one warm summer's day in July 2014. I'd had the novel idea among my creative thoughts for a few years about a girl, called Betsy Parker, who suffered an allergic condition that prevented her from being able to wear any clothes at all. However, I never thought the idea would evolve into a story, as the idea seemed too implausible. I have been involved in the naturist lifestyle since 2005 when I was 17 years old, and I suffer from Autism Spectrum Disorder, which has made it difficult for me to fit in with my peers. It was these two factors that inspired the idea, about how difficult it would be for someone to fit in who truly could never have any clothing on.

As the years passed, the story idea remained an idea, nothing more. It wasn't until the spring of 2014, when I was rummaging for something to write in my free time, when I remembered Betsy Parker, and decided to expand the idea into a synopsis. With a full-plot synopsis at hand, I expanded that synopsis into a novel the following summer, and completed the first draft in a swift six weeks.

To me, "The Sheltered Life of Betsy Parker" is not about a naked girl. It is not even, so much, about nudity itself. Rather, this novel is about struggle, acceptance, unconditional love and finding one's true self. Betsy Parker's clothes-free condition only serves as a vehicle for conveying these themes.

The reader might ask "Why pick a sensitive subject like nudity to use in conveying these themes?" I would answer with two reasons:

Firstly, almost invariably, the unclothed human form is either hidden beneath clothes, or is shown in demeaning, lustful, lewd, pornographic ways. Literature and films are often teeming with violence and profanity, while at the same time, censoring or going to great lengths to avoid any nudity at all of any kind. Then, if they do portray nudity, it's either done in a degrading, shameful, or lewd manner, or done as some kind of an embarrassing situation for the character who is unclothed. However, seldom does literature or a film write about, or show a completely unclothed human merely being naked, behaving just as casually as the person would if the person were wearing clothes. I believe that a novel focussing on nudity as simple, casual, and non-sexual serves to remind readers of the true way we are all born: naked, and completely innocent and unashamed in our nakedness. This is the way I have shown Betsy in this novel, as she grows from being a baby, to a toddler, to a school-age girl (homeschooled), to a young woman, living all these stages of life in nothing but her birthday suit.

Secondly, as the author, I am aware that I could cope with the struggle of the heroine through a real, existing disability, such as blindness, deafness, or being mentally or physically impaired. These conditions do present a struggle for those who suffer them, and could potentially trigger a storyline. However, I believe that the exotic, unique condition that affects Betsy would draw the reader into Betsy's world all the more, because her condition remains a condition that the reader can only imagine, and presents the optimal struggle for the heroine, not only because she is alone with it, but it's hard for her to even have people respect her because of it.

The reader might ask, "But why make her have to live her whole life completely naked? Can't you make it so that Betsy can, at least, wear clothing around her "private" parts, or have her find something obscure and unusual that she *can* use to clothe her body?"

I chose to have Betsy naked because, when questioning a taboo, either as a reader or as an author, one has to approach the issue face-to-face, rather than create ways to lessen the issue. The struggle that Betsy faces would lose impact and strength if she were able to find some way to clothe her way around her allergic condition. If Betsy were to be able to clothe her bum, vulva and breasts, or if she could find some rare material that doesn't affect her, it would only serve to reinforce the common societal belief that simple nudity is always something that has to be hidden, or that nudity can only ever be shown in a sexual manner.

I bear in mind the sensitive subject matter that this book depicts, so I have taken care to be sensitive to my readers. Hence, I only use nudity in this book in a naturist context, and I have limited themes of harsh language and violence only where truly necessary for the storyline. In doing so, I hope to maintain a balance between success for Betsy, and opposition against Betsy as she fights for success, acceptance and happiness throughout the novel.

Along with this book's underlying themes of acceptance, struggle, unconditional love and finding one's true self, I see a theme that proclaims the natural human form, not as indecent, but, rather, as a natural, beautiful, creative work of art; a family of body parts, making a complete person who can live, think, talk, laugh, play, and, most importantly ... love.

It is with great joy that I bring to you "The Sheltered Life of Betsy Parker."

38907151R00127

Made in the USA
San Bernardino, CA
15 September 2016